Praise for

Margaret of Thibodaux

"Jo Taylor's novel of a teenage summer bears all the qualities of the great literature of youth. . . . A masterclass in quality fiction writing, the plot is so artfully conceived that it calls into comparison some of the great coming-of-age novels of the twentieth century. Taylor's chapters, short and built around singular scenes and conversations between the principal characters, are some of the most organic and realistic moments this reviewer has encountered in recent fiction. At once humorous and deeply touching, elegantly plotted and rich in its construction of the characters, Taylor's novel is a stunning read by an author at the top of her craft."

—Stephen Dudas, PhD in Literature, *Reedsy Discovery*

". . . an intelligent and emotionally gratifying novel. . . . Author Jo Taylor has written a wonderful book with broad appeal."

—*Book Review Directory*

". . . its blend of Southern Gothic elements and evocative prose makes for a haunting yet deeply human coming-of-age story. At its core, Taylor's fiction debut is a story about true friendship, accepting cultural differences, and the unpredictable ways grief shapes—and ultimately frees—us."

—*BookLife*

Margaret
of
Thibodaux

Margaret of Thibodaux

A Novel

Jo Taylor

Road Clothes
PRESS

Copyright © 2025, Jo Taylor

All rights reserved. No part of this publication may be reproduced, distributed, or transmitted in any form or by any means, including photocopying, recording, digital scanning, or other electronic or mechanical methods, without the prior written permission of the publisher, except in the case of brief quotations embodied in critical reviews and certain other noncommercial uses permitted by copyright law. For permission requests, please address Road Clothes Press.

Published 2025
Printed in the United States of America
Hardcover ISBN: 978-1-962504-04-1
Paperback ISBN: 978-1-962504-05-8
Paperback ISBN: 978-1-962504-07-2
E-ISBN: 978-1-962504-06-5
Library of Congress Control Number: 2025900449

Road Clothes Press
Daphne, AL 36526
Roadclothespress.com

Editing and book design by Stacey Aaronson

This is a work of fiction. Names, characters, places, and incidents either are the product of the author's imagination or are used fictitiously. Any resemblance to actual persons, living or dead, is entirely coincidental.

NO AI TRAINING: Without in any way limiting the author's [and publisher's] exclusive rights under copyright, any use of this publication to "train" generative artificial intelligence (AI) technologies to generate text is expressly prohibited. The author reserves all rights to license uses of this work for generative AI training and development of machine learning language models.

To all the kids growing up with mad skills and to their parents who try to understand.

To my husband, Kevin, always the light on my way.

To my son, Jake, my one-eyed boy
(who has two very good and functional eyes).

To my dear friend, Kevin, who died when we were 18.
I still hear you laugh.

To my Dad, who made nitroglycerin and sarcasm.

To my Mom, who died when I was two,
but never left my side until I was grown up enough
to be the lady of the house.

Prologue

Sunday, April 7, 1968
Thibodaux, Louisiana

Daddy said I didn't need to go to Mama's funeral service at St. Joseph's Catholic Church.

We disagreed about that. Eight years old was not at all too young to attend a funeral, especially my own mama's.

I stared out our front window, my Sunday shoes rooted to the wooden parlor floor, and pressed my nose to the cool pane. I prayed to God to bring back Mama while Father Sean did the opposite—committed Mama back to God.

Grandma Betsy stayed behind with me at our great big house on Legard Street, but she spent the whole time in the kitchen, running water in the sink and banging pots around. Grandma was Daddy's mother, and she loved Mama, just like every one of us did.

The trees threw their dappled shade like it was any normal

day. They didn't have enough sense to know today was different. Birds perched up high, and a squirrel peeked around the bark of the oak tree across the street at the Getty house. The world should have stopped turning, but it just kept on.

I stood watch at the window for what seemed like hours until the grandfather clock in the hallway struck noon. Soon after, Daddy pulled into the drive in his silver Dodge Dart. He got out and stood still, swaying a bit like he didn't want to come in. But then Father Sean arrived and Daddy pushed away from the car, took off his hat, and fiddled with the brim as the priest walked up the drive. I saw them talking, then I hurried to the ladder-back cane chair at the entry to our formal living room. Wearing my best Sunday dress, I swung my feet while I sat on my white-gloved hands. Mama would be proud of me.

Daddy entered and gave me a somber smile. He dragged a chair up next to me and sat down. "The service is over," he said quietly. "Family and folks from town will be coming to our house now to give us condolences."

He didn't take the time to explain "condolences" like he usually did when I didn't know a word. Folks were already arriving. I rushed back to the window to see them parking their cars in a long line down our street. One by one, they got out carrying dishes of food and boxes wrapped in brown paper, so I figured condolences must be one of those things.

The sound of their car doors slamming shut reminded me of the time I saw what Daddy called a twenty-one-gun salute on TV. Everyone moved toward the house in slow motion, like they'd been called to the blackboard and didn't know the answer.

I hurried back to my chair once more and sat down. As everyone filed in, they kissed me on the head, patted my cheek, and said "sorry" a lot. One of the neighbor ladies said, "Margaret Thibodeaux, your mama would be so proud of you. Take good care of your daddy. You're the lady of the house now."

That seemed like a big responsibility. I looked down at my lap and placed my hands one on top of the other like a lady I saw posed on the cover of a magazine at the Piggly Wiggly, but it didn't make me feel grown up enough to be the lady of the house.

I watched the guests drift from group to group like the koi in Grandma Betsy's pond. They looked like fish too, with their eyes red and puffy and their lips moving without saying anything I understood. Mrs. Flint, Mrs. Browner, and the other Church Ladies made their way to the buffet and gathered in a semicircle, glancing my way in disdain. When my eyes met theirs, they quickly turned toward each other. They put gloved hands to their lips to block my view of their words, but I heard them just the same.

"Do you think it was intentional?"

"No," said Mrs. Flint, trying to take Mama's side. "It had to be an accident. It *was* an accident, right?"

Mrs. Browner, wearing her dirt-colored beeping hearing aids, whispered too loudly, "Well, if she did it on purpose, you know where she's going."

Other folks stopped talking and looked at me to see if I'd

heard. A tear rolled down my cheek. No one said a word, not in reprimand or agreement. The hush sat like a threat, painful and stealthy as ground fog, until Daddy strode in from the kitchen.

The Church Ladies swam off to the other side of the room. Daddy started to follow them but turned toward me instead. He handed me a glass of milk and knelt in front of me. His dark Acadian hair showed silvery-gray strands I'd never noticed before. I was more familiar with his shirt buttons and his voice than his eyes, cheeks, and hair.

"Are you all right?" he asked. "Want to go outside and play in the backyard with the other children?"

I shook my head. "No, sir. Not yet."

He wiped the tear from my cheek and took a deep breath. "Dr. King was buried today too."

"He was?"

Daddy nodded then stood to face the gathering. "President Johnson declared a National Day of Mourning today. I think it's appropriate."

The Church Ladies mumbled and raised tea glasses to their lips, then turned their backs to me. Fish.

"Daddy, did the president know Mama?" I asked.

He smiled and patted my shoulder. "No, Pea. The man who died the same day as Mama, he was important."

"Oh."

I took a drink of the cold milk and felt it go down, down, down, then set the glass on the table next to me. I pushed my fingers together to make my hands prayerful, even if my heart did not talk to God this time. It made sense that a king who was also a doctor was important. But Mama was my whole world.

Daddy walked over to The Fish and spoke in his quiet, serious voice. "Garbage is taken to the curb in this house."

"We didn't mean anything by it," Mrs. Browner said, her voice dripping with a sweetness that made me gag.

"Like hell, you didn't." Daddy's tone was soft and sharp at the same time. "Margaret heard you. I heard you. Everyone heard you."

The Fish grew quiet. Father Sean stepped in front of me and tried to form a barrier, but it was too late. Daddy moved out of Father Sean's eclipse and silently ushered Mrs. Browner out the front door.

Father Sean knelt beside me like Daddy had. "Sorry you had to hear all that."

"Did Mama . . ." I swallowed hard. "Is—was it—did I?"

The words didn't come out right, and I took big breaths to keep from crying.

"It's not for me to say," said Father Sean. It sounded like a practiced answer.

The way he left it open made me think about how I had disobeyed Mama the week before by climbing the tree in the backyard when I wasn't supposed to. How I didn't keep my room tidy. How on Monday I had left the dishes in the sink so long that Mama finally did them before Daddy got home. She had even scolded me for not doing my chores. Then, on that morning, the last one I saw Mama, I had rushed off to school, late again, and forgot to give her the birthday card I'd made for her.

"We buried her in consecrated ground," Father Sean added, "and we all pray she goes to heaven."

I stared at the little triangle sandwiches The Fish had brought, stacked in a pyramid. Father Sean was the second person to be unsure of her destination. I hadn't prayed for her safe arrival in Paradise when I said my prayers this morning. *God, please take her to heaven. Amen.*

Daddy returned and told me to eat something while he and Father Sean spoke in the kitchen, but I wasn't hungry. As I turned toward the parlor, a bright-flowered dress caught my eye. An older black woman I hadn't noticed before was sitting there alone. She raised her teacup in hello but didn't make a move to come talk to me. I wished everyone did that.

Just then, there was a knock at the door. Daddy opened it and invited the people in. A girl with golden hair, a boy a little older than her, and an older man entered the parlor.

"My name is Honey," the girl said. "You must be Margaret. I'm sorry about your mother." It sounded real, not practiced. I liked her right away.

"Thank you," I said.

"This is my pop and my brother, David."

Daddy had told me they'd be at the house today and that I might make a new friend. They had just moved in around the block on Second Street, one block from Bayou Lafourche, on the big corner lot with the pretty white house. He had also said David was a juvenile delinquent.

"Hi, Margaret," her pop said, "I'm sorry about your mama."

David smiled at me but said nothing, just raised his hand briefly like you do when the teacher calls roll.

"My mother couldn't come today," Honey lamented. "She said to tell you she's sorry."

The three of them flocked toward the gathering and introduced themselves. The Fish, Daddy's family from Tennessee, Mama's sisters from Mobile, and all the neighbors said their hellos. Honey was so at ease with new people. After several minutes, she broke away from the grown-ups and came over to me.

"Here, I brought you something," she whispered. She looked around as if she had something we would get in trouble for, then dropped a sugar cube into my hand. My gloves were too small, so they were tight like a drum and the cube almost bounced to the floor. I caught it before it escaped and we popped the cubes into our mouths at the same time. Our white Sunday gloves hid the evidence of thievery, and sugar was a better condolence than kisses and pats.

As I savored the cube in my mouth, the lady in the bright-flowered dress opened the door and disappeared.

Robert Pennington moved in next door about three weeks after Mama's funeral, near the first of May. On the very day he and his mother arrived, I rang their doorbell.

"My name's Margaret," I announced. "You want to play?"

Robert was two years older, and big for a ten-year-old.

"Sure," he said, then turned and yelled, "I'm going outside with Margaret!"

We walked around to his backyard, where the previous neighbors had kept their dog tied up all the time, so no grass grew near the back tree. A recent rain left a big mud puddle.

"Let's make mud pies," Robert said, adding a grin to his suggestion.

I shrugged like it was just a so-so idea, even though I thought it was brilliant.

We made the mud pies the size of hamburger patties.

"I'm gonna put these in the freezer next to the real hamburger," said Robert. "Mama won't know until they thaw out."

I laughed for the first time since the funeral. I loved him for that.

Mama came in one night during the first summer without her and sat on my bed, near my feet. It was like a heating pad on my leg, and the bed sank a little, but I wasn't afraid. Her perfume came to me, very faint, like when I'd snuck into her room and squirted a spray out of the bottle before getting scared and running back to my room.

I couldn't wait for her to come back the next night, but she didn't. It wasn't until a few nights later that I felt the bed sink again and I caught the smell of her perfume. I realized I couldn't predict when she would appear. But about a week later, on her third visit, she sang to me.

Go to sleepy, little baby.
Go to sleepy, little baby.
When you awake, you'll patty, patty-cake
and ride a shiny little pony.

In the fall, Grandma Betsy died. This time Daddy let me accompany him to her funeral at St. Joseph's Church. She was laid out and pasty in the casket and looked more like a plastic mannequin from Manci's department store than a person. I thanked God that I hadn't seen Mama in her casket.

Daddy and I said our last goodbyes to Grandma where they buried her in the cemetery. I expected Daddy to stop by Mama's grave and take flowers or talk to her for a bit, but instead he took my hand and led me back to the car.

Chapter 1

Saturday, June 8, 1974

I danced along the sidewalk on the way to Honey's house. A sidewalk should be flat, but this one disobeyed the rules. A live oak, planted too close, pushed up the concrete like paper, and pedestrians suffered as they tried to navigate the undulations without tripping. For me, though, it was easy.

Our small town of Thibodaux, the seat of Lafourche Parish, Louisiana, was sixty miles west of New Orleans. Some people lived here who'd never been to the big city. The bayou flowed through town like ink from a pen on its way to meet the delta of the Mississippi River to the southeast. The water was sometimes muddy, usually warm, and always moving. The whole of the town wasn't much above sea level and was as flat as the coastal plain could be.

Like all towns, Thibodaux set the base note of its people's

lives. It protected its own but passed judgment swiftly and without remorse. Steadfast in its view of hospitality and compassion as the hallmarks of humanity, it had very little crime. We played safely in the streets and by the bayou and got called home by whistles for supper from fathers, brothers, or, in Robert's case, mothers.

All the smells of summer arose on the way to Honey's: gardenias in Mrs. Fallon's yard, fresh-cut grass everywhere, and tuberoses—my favorite—in Honey's mother's garden.

Honey answered the door in a bright yellow dress with daisies on it that fell past her knees but would have been mid-thigh on me. "My room or outside?" she asked.

"Talking Tree," I said.

Honey pulled the door closed behind her, drawing pad and pencils in hand.

The Talking Tree was our spot. A half-mile from our block, next to the bayou, it sat right across the street from a big white house we called Tara because it looked just like the antebellum mansion in *Gone with the Wind*. Near the tree was an old swing set with three swings that probably belonged to the family who lived there, built for their children years ago. No one ever said we couldn't use them, though, so they seemed like ours.

We called it the Talking Tree because ever since we'd met, we would swing for hours, or sit under the shade of the tree when the summer sun beat us into submission, talking about life, school, family, and military history (Robert was a fan). When we needed to cool off, we moved down to the water's edge, where it was a pretty steep dropoff in some places, but in others was easy to inch down and put your feet into the water.

"I saw your daddy and Miss Muriel downtown the other day," said Honey. "They sure look googly-eyed at each other."

"I know. It's silly." I rolled my stiff shoulders. "She rubs me the wrong way."

"She does? Why?"

"She just does."

"Hm. Well, I like her. Do you think they're going to get married?"

"Heaven's no. Daddy tried the engagement thing once before, and it didn't work out well at all. He should be a bachelor from now on."

Honey paused for a moment. "Actually, he can't be a bachelor. He's a widower."

I shrugged. "Same thing."

Daddy would have appreciated Honey's correction. For a man who didn't work in an office, he had an extensive vocabulary. Whenever he used a word I didn't know and I asked him what it meant, he told me to look it up. The dictionary was so well-thumbed that it was impossible to tell from the closed book if Daddy had a favorite letter. He even did spelling tests with me during the summer to augment what I learned in school. "You must learn to read, write, and speak your own language," he reasoned. In actuality, it wasn't a reason so much as a commandment, but he lived by it, so I could too.

It got me into uncomfortable situations, my vocabulary.

The kids at school teased me for using big words, but because I was friends with Honey—and she was smart in so many things—I used her as my excuse. Luckily, she didn't mind. She couldn't care less about teasing. Plus, seventies words didn't do anything for Honey or me, and the slang of the day never passed our lips. It became a badge of courage to refrain from talking like everybody else.

I wasn't interested in math or physics, but words—that was a subject I could get lost in all day. My favorite word was "obstreperous," which basically means being a pain in the ass. After Daddy's booming voice said it in my direction one day, my word for him became "draconian," although he never was.

I sank into the cool grass and stretched out along the lovely blanket nature had made. "What are we going to do this summer?"

Honey did a freedom twirl with her arms out like a propeller. "I think we should draw, and skip rope, and read, and solve the problems of the world."

When I didn't respond, Honey plopped down next to me. "Hey," she prodded, giving my shoulder a shove.

"Don't you think she's too perfect?" I said, staring up at the sky.

"Who?"

"You know who."

"Oh, Muriel. No such thing. Besides, your daddy seems happy. Don't you want him to be happy?"

"Not at my expense, no." I picked blades of grass, tearing them in half and half again. "Besides, what if she decides to leave after I've spent time getting used to her? Rachel Patrick's had three stepmothers already."

"You're being unfair. Plus, you can't judge anything by what happens in the Patrick family."

I sat up on my elbows. "That's true . . . but Muriel's fake."

"Fake? How?"

"Hey, Robert!" I called out.

Honey jumped a mile as she usually did when I sensed Robert was around before either of us saw him.

I swiveled to see Robert break into a run a hundred yards from where we sat. It took only seconds before he reached us.

"What are my two best girls talking about?" he asked.

We exchanged glances then stared at our shoes.

"Great. I love stare-at-my-shoes Saturday." Robert dropped onto the grass next to us. "Seriously, I saw you talking and now nothing?"

I shrugged. If I tried to describe our disagreement, I would sound whiny. I worked on it all the time, my voice, but my tendency to exaggerate brought another component to the whiny equation. I let my silence provoke Honey to speak.

"We were talking about her daddy and Miss Muriel and how I like her and Margaret doesn't."

Robert laughed. "That's none of my business for sure, and probably not either of yours."

We glared at him, caught between his truth and our egos.

I let it go first and ambled over to the middle swing, the prized spot for never getting left out of a conversation. I pulled the pony band I always wore on my wrist around my unruly dark hair and began pumping my long legs forward and back. Honey and Robert joined me.

Honey's real name was Annabelle Jane, but her father called her Honey from the time she was two because of her curly blond hair. Her folks had been Southern for generations, from Georgia, not Louisiana. Catholic, but not French Catholic like the Cajuns and like me. She was flighty, happy, ethereal, smart, and the most thoughtful human I'd ever known. I never figured out how one person got so much blessing from up above, but I put it down to the fact that Honey must have deserved it.

Robert's heritage, in contrast to ours, was a mix of African, Spanish, and French, and he was proud of it—his people had been living in Louisiana since before it was part of the United States. His Creole skin was a warm golden brown, like he was always tan. I envied his color against my pale, strictly French-descended skin.

"We were also talking about what to do this summer," I said. "Any ideas?"

Robert was a simple guy. "I vote for fishing, playing cops and robbers, and catching lightning bugs. But my mama wants me to work at the Piggly Wiggly. I'm gonna try to get out of it, though."

"Oh, you have to!" Honey pleaded. "We won't have any fun if you have to work!"

"Yeah, but Mama says sixteen means no more running around doin' nothing. I guess she's right, but I'd really like one more year of an actual summer."

"You should sweet-talk her," Honey said. "Tell her you have to be our protector. She likes us and wouldn't want us to be stuck at home because you're not around."

"That's a prime idea," Robert said. "I'll see what I can do."

Honey smiled and tipped her face upward. Her golden hair whipped around in the breeze.

Robert jumped from the swing, followed by Honey and then me. Together, we made an odd set: two girls and a boy, two tall and one short. Perfect.

"Wanna fish?" Robert asked.

Usually Honey said, "No way," but she surprised me by saying "Sure!" with more enthusiasm than she'd ever had for my ideas, like roller skating or riding bikes. So, fishing was the first official thing we did for summer.

Robert ran the few blocks home while we waited near the Talking Tree. When he returned, sweat dripped from his brow as he handed me a pole and a box of lures. He hooked Honey's pole up first, then mine, then his.

"Maybe we'll be going to a wedding this summer," Honey teased.

"Not funny, Miss Sinclair."

Robert cast his line. "What's so bad about your daddy getting married?"

"I don't need a new mother," I said. "I have one. She's just dead, that's all."

What I didn't say was that Mama came to visit me all the time, and if Miss Muriel came into our lives to stay, Mama might leave forever.

After a few hours, Daddy's whistle cut through the warm Gulf air.

"Gotta go," I said. I reeled in my line, pried off the hook, and set the rod on the bank. "See you guys tomorrow."

As I started toward home, I pivoted to wave. But Robert and Honey were sitting side by side at the bayou's edge, looking at each other.

"Bye," I called to them.

"Bye," they both answered without looking my way.

Ever since the first time Mama came to me after she died, she'd never been far away. I didn't even need to hear Mama sing or smell her perfume to know it was her. I can't tell you how I knew. I just did. When I'd told Daddy that Mama came to my room at night, he just patted my head and nodded. I'd learned not to tell him about the other presences in the house or the sounds around me everywhere. He'd moved from tolerating, if not accepting, my "imaginary" sensations to qualifying them as bullshit on occasion. Now, at fourteen, I hadn't mentioned anything to him for two years and I was certain he thought I'd grown out of it.

Most of the time, I paid no mind to the sensations. I assumed that if it wasn't Mama, it was a spirit of some sort, but they didn't scare me or invade my space. I felt presence, but saw nothing. I heard sounds that I attended to when I wanted, but easily shut out when I was otherwise engaged. Sometimes, it sounded like a group of people whispering. When I was younger, I would look around and even go outside to the garage or the back tree, searching for someone talking. But over time, I learned to recognize the "Sph sp sp wh sh sh" as a spirit voice, and it only bothered me when I tried to sleep and the voices *not* in my head wouldn't shut up.

In catechism, I remembered the Church saying you shouldn't try to communicate with spirits, not that it wasn't possible. The Church said you only talked to demons, but I didn't buy it. If demons talked to you, so did regular spirits.

I never interacted with Mama or any of the other voices or presences; they simply coexisted in my world. It never occurred to me to communicate back, a small level of deference to the Church's teachings. But if Muriel stayed in our lives, this would have to change.

I wanted everything to stay the same, and I knew they wouldn't if Daddy got married. What scared me most was the thought that Mama would get pushed out by Muriel being with Daddy. I couldn't let that happen, so I was prepared to push Muriel away rather than risk never feeling Mama again.

In the past few weeks, Daddy had spent a lot more time with Muriel. He not only talked about her more, but I noticed that the pictures and memories of Mama in the house were no longer there. He never mentioned her things, and I wasn't sure how he would respond if I asked about them.

When I finally mustered the courage to inquire where Mama's photos and belongings had gone, he blandly responded from behind his newspaper, "Did you try the garage and the attic?"

"Yes, sir. I didn't find anything."

"Hmm."

I asked more questions, but all he said was, "Not now, Margaret."

My boldness grew. "I'm distressed at this arrangement," I said, still talking to the back of the paper.

He remained buried in the news, which meant he wasn't in the mood for an inquisition. "You need to pay more attention. I'm sure they're all here somewhere."

I threw my hands on my hips, not that Daddy noticed. "That doesn't make any sense. How can I pay attention to something I can't find in the first place?"

His silence was my answer.

I shifted my attention to Muriel. I realized I needed to figure out if Mama disappearing from the house had something to do with her or if Daddy was doing it for himself. Mama's pictures, her perfume, all of her things had sat on her dresser for six years. Now they were gone.

As I neared our house, I wished I could talk to Honey and Robert about Mama, but how do you tell your friends your dead Mama comes to visit you?

I strode up the front porch steps and turned the handle on the great front door. "I'm home," I called into the kitchen.

"Almost ready," Daddy called back. "Go wash up and change."

Daddy cooked dinner on Saturdays for us since I did the weekdays. He'd graduated from the awful TV dinners in the early years after Mama died to a pretty acceptable gumbo, fine steaks, and the occasional pot pie. He wore the Betty Crocker apron when he made the pie dough, but promised to break the camera if I ever took a picture of him in it.

After washing my hands, brushing my hair, and changing the shirt that had fish guts near the front hem, I bounded down the stairs. The unmistakable aroma of fried catfish greeted me at the bottom.

"How was the first day of summer?" Daddy asked as I slid into my chair. He always started with a "How was" question. Predictable.

"Pretty good. We went to the Talking Tree and then fished. Standard summer stuff."

Daddy placed a bowl of vegetable soup in front of each of us. I began slurping it down. It was salty and perfect.

Daddy rolled his eyes.

"What? Slurping is a sign of respect in China. You tell me to eat everything on my plate because there are starving kids in China. Well, they would slurp."

"We don't live in China," he reminded me. "Please don't do that."

"Yes, sir." I opted to pour the soup into my mouth with my spoon, but I'd rather have slurped it.

We were silent until I finished, then I said, "I looked for the pictures of Mama in your bedroom closet. They weren't there."

"Oh?" he said. "The sideboard in the parlor, then?"

"Not there either." I squirmed slightly. "Did you throw them away, Daddy?"

"Of course not, Pea. I must have put them away in such a safe place that now we can't find them." He smiled to soften my glare.

"Pea" was short for "Sweet Pea," a name Mama gave me because I was so tiny when I was born—the size of a pea pod. Daddy took to calling me Pea after Mama died, and I'd never decided if I liked it or not.

"But why would you do that? Now there are no pictures in this house of Mama, no memories, no nothing."

His eyes glued to his last spoonfuls of soup, he said, "No reason. I just started putting old things away."

"But Daddy. Mama isn't any old thing."

He took in a breath, as if someone had just poked him with something sharp. Then he rose to get the plates of fish. I waited for him to answer, but he returned to the table with his eyes downcast, then flaked the catfish with his fork.

All during the meal, Daddy didn't say another word to me. When he took his plate into the kitchen, I announced I was going to my room.

"Aren't you going to—" His voice trailed off.

I usually offered to wash dishes when he cooked, but not tonight. I stomped up the stairs to send Daddy the message that I was displeased, even though the carpeted steps muffled this communication.

Later that night, as I emerged from the gauzy haze of sleep, I felt Mama sitting on the bed at my feet. I sat up, thrilled that she had come when I needed to talk to her. But either the motion, or the conscious thought, made Mama's presence disappear.

Chapter 2

Saturday, June 15, 1974

The community pool opened at 11:00 a.m., and Honey, Robert, and I met outside the gates at ten thirty. We planned to go on the hottest days and had gotten ten-punch cards so we'd have ten trips for the summer.

Honey and I both had had swimming lessons for years and were comfortable in the water. But Robert had started lessons just last year and was decidedly less sure. Most of the time, though, no one swam because there were so many people in the pool. I liked to dive under the water, imagining I was a mermaid with an elegant silvery-green tail that whacked the water whenever I surfaced.

During the rest times, we ate soft, salted pretzels with mustard and drank a Coke, the only time I could have one since Daddy did not approve nor buy them. Back in the pool, we played catch and did tricks and came out pickled by four thirty when the last whistle blew. We changed clothes in the locker room and hurried to our bikes for the fifteen-minute ride home because supper was at five for all of us.

When I got to my house, Muriel's car was in the drive. Daddy was a stickler for punctuality, so I hoped he wouldn't notice I was a little late. When I scurried into the dining room, Muriel was seated at the table wearing a pretty pink dress and a ribbon to tie up her dark brown hair.

Daddy and I always sat across from each other. He was unusually democratic in that regard, not insistent on being at the head of the table to prove he was the head of the family. Even when Mama was alive, he sat next to her and across from me. But tonight, to his right, Muriel was in the chair Mama used to sit in.

I'd kept count of the nine times she'd been at our house before tonight. Number ten had already put a pit in my stomach, and I fell into my chair as if I weighed a thousand pounds.

I crossed myself and started eating. Daddy cleared his throat, and I glanced up to find both of them staring at me.

"I'm sorry I'm late, Daddy, but it's only five minutes. It won't happen again." I looked down at my plate, not able to maintain eye contact with his steely blues.

But instead of being upset with me, he said, "We have something to tell you."

I peered across the table to see Daddy's fingers tapping the edge of his plate and on Muriel's finger, a ring. On her *left* hand. I jerked my head up.

Daddy smiled. "So you see it. The ring."

Muriel said something too but it didn't register. My only

perception was an incessant *No, No, No, No, No* running through my head.

"We're engaged," Daddy clarified, as if I needed to hear the words. "Muriel is my fiancée."

I stood up, tipping the chair wildly behind me. "I'm not hungry anymore."

Daddy wasn't having it. "Sit down." His voice was sharp. "Don't you have anything else to say, like congratulations?"

"No." I felt myself teetering and had to press my fingertips into the tabletop to steady myself.

Daddy gave Muriel a pleading look. "I'm sorry. I don't know what's wrong. Would you mind going to the kitchen and getting more potatoes?"

Muriel picked up the already full potato bowl and excused herself to the kitchen.

Daddy leaned toward me on his elbows and hissed in a low voice, "What is wrong with you?"

"I don't like her," I hissed back.

"You never said anything these last six months."

"Well, I didn't know you were going to make it permanent. I was just going to skate through like I did with all the others."

Daddy winced at that. There had only been two others. I let the exaggeration stand.

"We'll talk about this later," he said. "But you must mind your manners no matter what. I will not tolerate you being mean to her. Understand? She's a kind, loving, thoughtful woman."

I wanted to roll my eyes but thought better of it. "Yes, sir. May I be excused?"

Daddy rubbed his brow with his middle finger. "Yes, but only to gather your composure. Got it?"

"Yes, sir."

I raced up the stairs and slammed my bedroom door.

Daddy had proposed once before to a teacher at the college, but she'd disappeared like a firefly at sunrise at the sight of a ring. He'd taken it hard, slamming doors and even yelling at me when I dropped a dish on the kitchen floor. After a few days of miserable Daddy, I snuck into his bedroom and saw the ring on his nightstand, looking bereft. I moved it to the box in the bottom drawer that held Mama's ring and a lock of my hair. I noticed that he relaxed when it didn't stare at him anymore. Two rings in the drawer beat an outsider in our home.

Daddy had tried hard to move on from Mama's death, but I hadn't.

I stood in front of my dresser. Mama's picture, the one of her at the park with me when I was just a baby, sat in the very center, the place of honor. I picked up the heavy silver frame and held it close, wishing something simple could bring Mama to me. She was far away, and I blamed Muriel.

A knock on the door alerted me to Daddy's tall frame in the doorway. He didn't ask to enter, just slipped in and closed the door behind him.

"I'd like you to come back down and join us," he said gently but firmly. "This is supposed to be a celebration."

I clung tighter to Mama's photo. "I don't feel like celebrating your *fiancée*." The word stuck in my throat like a fish bone. I hadn't considered his life going on without Mama, without me.

"Margaret, be reasonable. She's lovely and kind, and she makes my world light up."

"Downstairs she was thoughtful too."

"You're on the edge, young lady."

I took a step back from him, holding the picture against my chest like armor.

"What about my world? Doesn't that count for anything? Doesn't the list of pros need to be valuable for both of us?"

"In this case, no. And I don't understand why you would object to Muriel—or be so rude to her so publicly."

I lowered the picture ever so slightly. "Publicly? We aren't in public. We're in our house and I'll be rude if I feel like it."

"So you *were* being rude on purpose."

He'd baited me into confessing my sin.

Daddy squeezed his arms at his sides, as if to control his body's reaction to my words. "It's *my* house, not ours. And let me disabuse you of the notion you have the right to be rude if you feel like it, especially when there's a guest in this house. You don't. Not ever. I expect you to engage in civil discourse, *always*. Is that understood?"

"Yes, sir," I mustered.

"And don't ever be rude to Miss Muriel again. Mama would hate it."

He knew I loathed doing anything that would make Mama unhappy and used that against me.

"Mama would hate you marrying someone else."

Daddy sighed. "The vows say ''til death do us part,' Margaret. I have a right to be happy."

"Well, so do I."

Daddy was done with our *civil discourse*. "Yes, well, right now I expect you downstairs. So compose yourself and be down in two minutes." He turned to leave then faced me again. "And be nice. It's not that hard." He disappeared into the hall, closing the door behind him.

All I wanted was to feel Mama, to get guidance on how to deal with Daddy in love and a woman I barely knew wanting to come into our home.

I waited the whole two minutes then banged my door closed on my way out so they could hear it downstairs. I pretended I was a debutante and assumed a regal posture for my entrance. It was a wasted effort, though. Muriel and Daddy were staring at each other, holding champagne glasses, and didn't even look my way.

I sat down and stared at my plate. The food was still arranged as I'd left it ten minutes ago, but a champagne flute now sat to the right of it. It was half full, but champagne nonetheless. *Bribery.*

Daddy met my eyes with a look that said he expected me to heed his instructions. I'd shown him evidence of composure when I walked into the room. It wasn't my fault he'd missed it.

Muriel spoke first. "I think we surprised you. Sorry. I'm looking forward to getting to know you better."

My turn. "Yes, I *am* surprised. I'm sorry if I was rude." I did not return the "looking forward to getting to know you better" sentiment.

Daddy must have felt this was good enough. Raising his glass, he said, "To Muriel. To us."

Muriel stared into Daddy's eyes. They both ignored me when I raised my glass and said, "To Louisiana." I drank the champagne in one gulp, hoping the bubbles would counteract the heavy feeling in my chest. It was fruity and sweet, a surprise that tasted like silver.

Daddy laughed and said, "Champagne is for sipping." Then he smiled at me, maybe to take the edge off his correction when I couldn't possibly have known how to do it right.

By the end of dinner, I was more relaxed. My head was now bubbly, and my body was too. Daddy stepped out on the back porch to smoke, leaving me stuck with Muriel. Neither one of us spoke, just glanced around the room and at our hands. When our eyes met, she smiled. I didn't.

Daddy and I never talked much before Mama died, and afterward, in the early years, the evenings were stiff with:

"How was your day?"

"Fine."

"Good."

Back then, there'd been a picture of Mama on top of the TV set. I never knew if his attention was on her or the TV. Either way, we sat quietly each evening while fifty thousand things swirled in my head when I wasn't supposed to talk. Sometimes a few came out anyway, and I could always tell he was annoyed by the way he sighed and rubbed his eyebrow.

This, though, was a different situation. This was a grown-up conversation setting. I pondered my future and hoped my adult conversations would not be this awkward and uncomfortable.

Muriel broke the silence. "Margaret, will you be a bridesmaid for me?"

"What?" I blurted out before I could stop it.

"A bridesmaid," she repeated with a slight smile.

Oh no. A direct question that required an answer. I weighed the consequence of saying no, imagining a tirade from Daddy and tears from Muriel, then a stone coldness that would never break, no matter how much I tried to make amends.

Muriel gave it a third try. "Will you be my bridesmaid? I'll buy you a pretty pink dress and everything."

I couldn't imagine anything worse. "Yes, ma'am."

When Daddy came back into the dining room, he and Muriel began clearing the table. I didn't get up to help.

On Daddy's last trip into the room to get the champagne flutes and butter dish, I asked if I could be excused. He'd forgotten to dismiss me, and I was following the rules to the letter now.

"Of course you may."

As I stood up to leave, he asked, "What did you and Miss Muriel talk about?"

"She wants me to be a bridesmaid."

"I know." His face turned into a sappy smile. "It's so thoughtful of her."

"It is?"

Daddy looked puzzled. "She's already planned to take you next Saturday."

"Take me where?"

"Dress shopping. Downtown."

I tried to appear pathetic, like the little kids in the Save the Children commercials. "Don't you think this is all a bit—fast?"

"What do you mean?"

I tried to tread the "rude" line just right. "First you get engaged and then suddenly I'm in the wedding. I'm not even sure I want to be." I waited for the consequences.

"I think you should just be silent on this whole topic."

"Silence is fine, Daddy. You used to prefer it."

Chapter 3

Sunday, June 16, 1974

For the first time in my life, I did not follow the rules.
Dixit Dominus
Domino meo
Sede ad dextris meis

As the priest intoned the Latin words, his voice floated above my head to the loveliest ceiling in existence. The architect must have spent years designing St. Joseph's so that everyone sounded heavenly, even Father Archibald. We were lucky to have such a stunning church. Most Catholics spent Sundays in their small, ordinary town church, but we lived near an actual cathedral—a high-ceilinged, bright, stained-glass, knock-em-dead showstopper.

Rosary in hand, *Ave Maria, Gratia Plena*, I didn't count the beads to keep a prayerful place. Instead, I counted the faults of Muriel Lafleur, Daddy's newly minted fiancée. *Helmet hair. Batty eyelashes. Pink lipstick. Pink shoes. Pink dress. Soft voice.* I was going to run out of beads.

After Mama's funeral, I wasn't too keen on returning to Mass, because of all the whispers. One Sunday, outside the cathedral, I caught The Fish talking about Mama. Mrs. Browner was uttering the same filthy lie she had the day of the funeral, that Mama had "surely gone to hell for what she did"—and she continued spreading the story as new fish joined the group. I had made my presence known with a cough and a glare that would have wilted a sunflower at noon, but The Fish just turned away. I had picked up the cross of the smoldering feud, reserving church for Christmas, Easter, and when I needed something. I wanted to love the Church, but its Fish didn't love my family. The only reason I attended now was because Honey came with me. After Daddy's announcement last night, I figured only she or God could help me.

Daddy never attended Mass anymore either. He'd gone back to attending the Episcopal church a few blocks away, which is where he met Muriel six months ago. He told me he noticed her for longer than that but was afraid she'd never see anything in a man who picked up garbage for a living. He was wrong.

I ticked through the remaining beads. *Cold hands. Fake laugh. Beady eyes. Mississippi drawl. Episcopalian. Miss Clairol 120. Petite. Doctor. Painted nails.* When I ran out of faults, "Mama would spit nails" became the mantra. The thought boomed in my head so loudly that I was afraid Honey heard it. When she glared at me, I guessed she was confused as to why I was saying the rosary during Mass.

When I glanced up from my beads, St. Ignatius of Loyola,

the patron saint of admonishing sinners, stared at me. At catechism, dressed in his armor, he seemed critical of us, and I'd asked Sister Mary about him. Too bad The Fish didn't understand who watched over them at Mass.

Father Archibald began the reading, and I sat back in the pew with the practiced face of paying attention while my mind wandered to things besides Abram and Lot. Honey always insisted we sit near the front and in the center, but I'd learned early on that if I sat behind one of the giant pillars, Father Archibald couldn't see me. It didn't matter when you were in church if the priest could see you or not because Jesus and God were everywhere, but today I was on full display for everyone.

If Mama had killed herself and gone to hell, how had she sung lullabies to me all these years? I wondered. Mama *must* be mad that she was being replaced.

"He who does justice will live in the presence of the Lord," I answered without caring what the words meant.

Father said a few lines, and the congregation replied again, "He who does justice will live in the presence of the Lord."

I squeezed my eyes shut and wished Muriel would go away.

"He who does justice will live in the presence of the Lord."

I did *not* want a stepmother.

"He who does justice will live in the presence of the Lord."

If I could have crawled out of my skin, I would have. I bounced my legs, trying to get the frustration out of my system, probably looking like I was having a seizure. Honey glared at me again and gave me a concerned nudge. I'd been late this morning and didn't have time to even say hello, let alone to tell her the news. Even though Honey worshipped Miss Muriel for reasons I couldn't fathom, I knew she would rally to my side in my time of need.

I stuffed the rosary in my pants pocket. The only time I wore regular pants was to church—my halfway point to wearing a dress. I fidgeted with the beads beneath the material, then graduated to scratching at the wood grain of the pew as the congregation continued their Catholic calisthenics of singing, kneeling, standing, responding.

Finally, the priest said, "Peace be with you."

I jerked my head up when Mrs. Flint turned from the pew in front of me to "offer each other the sign of peace." Mrs. Flint was the most decent of The Fish, but I still offered my hand in the weakest, limpest way possible to not really mean I wished peace on her. At least Mrs. Browner was floating two rows away on the left side of the aisle, out of reach.

Communion was my opportunity to express my needs, when God was closest.

"Body of Christ."

"Amen."

On my prayerful way back to my seat, I noticed the flowers in the altar arrangement smelled like jasmine, though I didn't see any trailing from the bouquet. I said the required words in my head. The choir in the loft sang softly, except for the one voice that always badgered the rest. The Body was sweet on my tongue, and I let it sit there as I wondered how Jesus fit into this tiny circle.

I knelt in the pew. While others in the congregation reflected on their desire to be a better person, I let God have it.

Please don't let this happen. I don't want a stepmother. I'll be good, I promise. Please make her go away or get sick. No, wait, I don't want her sick. If I let Daddy get married, I'll have to be nice to her forever, and I don't think I can do it. You might not like me trying to feel Mama all the time, but I'm so afraid that if Muriel comes to live with us, Mama will never come around again. I don't think I could stand it. So, please, make this whole thing go away. And could you make it happen before I have to go shopping for a bridesmaid dress? I'd like an answer soon, but it might take you a little while. Please hurry. Amen.

I admit, I expected an angel from heaven to bring my answer from God on a silver scroll.

When the priest dismissed us, Mrs. Browner stood at the front doors and sneered at me as she handed me a flyer for the youth group titled "How to Obey Your Parents." I would not be attending that function.

The church bells rang noon as I sat on the bench near the statue of St. Joseph, watching the scuttling clouds overhead with the sun casting rays of light through them near my feet, waiting for Honey as she talked to the priest, the deacon, and The Fish. When Honey finally got to me, she immediately scolded, "What's wrong with you? I'm sure Father Archibald noticed you this morning."

"Why, hello, Miss Honey," I said, admonishing her for the sin of her improper greeting. "So nice to see you this morning. How are you this fine day?"

She sat beside me. "Sorry. Hi, Margaret. How are you?"

"What's wrong and how am I? I can answer both at the same time. Daddy and Miss Lafleur are engaged."

Honey drew in a loud breath and clapped her hands. She hugged me and squealed, "Oh, you are so lucky! That's wonderful news!"

I pulled away and let my shoulders fall. "Wonderful news? Um, *no*, it's not."

Honey looked crestfallen, as if she'd misunderstood the rules of a game. "Why is it not good news?"

"I can't believe you would even ask. I thought you of all people would understand that I don't need a new mother. I have one. Just because she's dead doesn't mean she isn't still my mother."

"True," Honey said. "But you don't mind when my mother does things for you—like giving you hot chocolate on a rainy day. What if Miss Muriel mothers you like that?"

I smoldered at Honey's ability to clip my concerns into little bits. "She's taking me shopping for a *bridesmaid's* dress," I said, sure that she couldn't possibly support Miss Muriel in ignoring my distaste for girlish attire.

"Oh. Do people die from shopping for a bridesmaid's dress?" Honey asked.

That did it. I abruptly stood and turned my back to her, then marched out of the courtyard toward home.

Within seconds, Honey skipped up beside me. We got three blocks, to the corner of Lagarde and Fourth Street, before I calmed down and stopped marching like the sidewalk had it coming. As I settled into a lazy walk, I noticed the scent of roses that hung over fences, and gardenias too.

"What are we doing today?" Honey asked.

Southern girls disliked confrontation, and we were both expert at deploying any tactic we could think of to avoid it.

"I need to learn how to talk to Mama," I said.

"That's easy. You can pray." Honey picked an errant daisy that poked way over its fence, then plucked the petals one by one.

"That's not what I mean. Praying is so one-sided. Everyone says you'll get an answer, but really, you have to make up an answer yourself and say it's from God."

"Then what are you talking about?"

"Talking to *her*. Like actually talking. Her, me, both of us communicating."

"Um, I don't think that's possible."

I swung around to face her. "Aha! I know something more than you do! The Church says you *shouldn't* do it, not that it's *impossible*."

"And what part of 'shouldn't' don't you understand? You always follow the rules. You won't even cross the street unless the light is green."

"Father Archibald still says part of Mass in Latin, and *he's* not supposed to. So I should be able to talk to Mama."

Honey laughed.

I gave her the dodgeball enemy glare. "What's so funny?"

"Me. I'm funny. I gave you the perfect setup for making your point, complete with clergy disobeying the rules."

I tipped my head in confusion.

"Oh, never mind. The point is, you've upped your game, Miss Margaret. This should be a *very* interesting summer."

I was hanging on the way she stretched out the word *very* when I saw Robert turn the corner ahead of us.

"Hey!" I shouted.

Robert turned around. "Hey!" he called back.

When we caught up to him, the three of us walked single file down the narrow, cracked sidewalk.

"Let's see if I have better luck this time," he said. "What are my two best girls talking about?"

"Priests," I said.

"We were also talking about catechism," Honey added.

Robert was Catholic too, but his mama didn't make him go to church except on Easter and Christmas, like me. "What's so fascinating about that?"

"Spirits."

"Holy Spirits?" he asked.

"No, just regular spirits."

"What about 'em?"

Honey swiveled and faced him square, walking backward. "Do you think you can talk to spirits, that it's possible?"

"Well, I can't, but I think it's possible. Mama's family has some folks who swear they can talk to spirits whenever they want. Kinda creepy."

"See," I said to Honey.

"See what?" Robert asked.

"Margaret's daddy is going to marry Miss Lafleur, and Margaret wants to talk to her mama about . . . what *do* you want to talk to her about, anyway?"

I felt my face flush. "I, well, I . . . I don't know." I wasn't prepared to present my reasons yet; the idea was still zigzagging through my mind. "Mary Kate Le Blanc has a stepmother, and she hates her. Did you know she makes her wear a bib at the table that says 'I'm a Pig' if she's messy at supper the night before? Can you imagine the humiliation? I'd be wearing the damn thing all the time."

"Ohhh," Honey said in a placating tone. "Miss Muriel isn't like that at all. I think she's lovely. I also think you shouldn't try to contact spirits, even your mama. What if you end up talking to the devil himself?"

I stopped. "I'd ask him if it's hot down there."

Honey crossed herself and Robert laughed while I skipped ahead of them toward home.

Our church clothes stuck to our bodies like jam to biscuits by the time we got to my house. I changed quickly into play clothes, then stopped at Honey's so she could change too. We nabbed slices of watermelon from Honey's kitchen for all three of us, then proceeded to the Talking Tree. Nothing was as satisfying on a hot day as that sweet, chilled, watery red stuff.

We each grabbed a swing and spit seeds as we ate, competing in both accuracy and distance.

"Hey, guys," I said. "I have a question for you." My tone got their attention.

"Yeah?" they said in unison.

"I feel like I'm betraying Mama if I'm okay with Daddy and Miss Muriel getting married."

"That's not a question," Honey said. "That's a declarative sentence."

"Honey Jane, you know what I mean. Is it *wrong* to feel like I'm betraying Mama if I accept it?"

"Doesn't seem to me like you have much choice," Honey said. "I think you're making an awful big deal out of it."

"'Til death do us part,'" Robert said. "Your mama's dead. Your daddy doesn't owe her anything, and neither do you. I doubt she gives a rat's ass."

"But . . ." I'd expected more commiseration with my predicament. "You're saying you think I should give in and not stand up for Mama?"

"Is it your mama you're standing up for?" Honey asked.

It stung a little that Honey wasn't seeing things my way. "Daddy put all her pictures away."

"All of them?" Honey asked, a tremor in her voice.

"Yeah," I said with a shrug, "but I guess I'm just making an awful big deal out of it."

Honey and Robert exchanged a glance.

"Gosh, Margaret," said Honey. "That sounds terrible. I'm sorry. Is that why you're so against Miss Muriel?"

I hopped off the swing and walked the fifteen steps to the edge of the bayou. I sat on the cool grass and slipped off my sneakers, dipping my toes into the muddy water. They joined me, but we sat in silence, an end to the Muriel conversation.

Honey never liked it when the conversation stopped, so she'd usually ask our opinion on something to keep it going. A Southern girl isn't supposed to have an opposing opinion on anything; we always let whomever we're talking to think theirs is the right one. Frankly, I never understood how the South made any progress that way.

In this case, the topic of Daddy's impending marriage to a woman I couldn't bear being a constant part of your lives was, at least temporarily, put on the back burner.

"Robert, what's your favorite virtue?" Honey asked, starting a new interrogation à la Proust.

"Beer."

Honey slapped her knee. "Beer is *not* a virtue."

"For some people, it's their only redeeming value. That makes it a virtue."

I admired how Robert used peculiar logic in his favor.

"No, really," Honey said. "What kind of virtue do you like the most in yourself or other folks?"

He tipped his head in thought. "Honesty. But that's a boring answer."

"It's not boring," Honey said in a tone I'd never heard from her before. "Margaret, what about you?"

"I'll take kindness for one hundred dollars."

Honey rolled her eyes. "We aren't playing *Jeopardy*."

Robert laughed.

"Oh all right," I said. "Let me think." I stifled a giggle. "I think patience is the best virtue."

"Good thing," Robert said.

We would push Honey over the edge someday. I knew it.

Robert surprised me by bringing the conversation back to my dilemma. "If you want to talk to your mama so bad, what about going to see Jezebel?"

I glanced at Honey, wide-eyed. She would *not* support me if I pursued help from the Voodoo Woman.

"I went up the walk once, and when I got close to her house, it smelled like fried chicken," Robert said. "I don't see how there can be anything wrong with someone who eats fried chicken."

"Agreed," I said. "Assuming it's chicken."

Robert pursed his lips at me like everyone did.

The rumor was that Jezebel was a Voodoo Priestess. She lived in a shotgun-style house, the roof missing a few shingles, the back-left corner covered in moss, but tidy and clean. It stood under the shade of an oak tree hundreds of years old, its branches bent all the way to the ground. Painted yellow with white trim and a red door, the house's outward-facing brightness belied its dark intrigue. She kept the window shades pulled down all day and night, which meant that only scant light escaped the interior. To add to the mystery, she mostly stayed indoors. But on those occasions—according to rumor—when she came outside to cut herbs from her window boxes or sit in the singular white rocker on her porch, kids would scatter in fear. Their descriptions of her matched a storybook demon more than they matched a middle-aged black woman.

Jezebel held an ominous presence in the neighborhood, mainly because those same middle-school kids made up ever more elaborate stories to scare each other. Honey and I had passed her house hundreds of times, yet never saw her once. She didn't even leave her door or windows open like everybody else when the breeze was nice in early spring and fall.

I sometimes wondered if Jezebel even existed. Robert's idea of her helping me talk to Mama sat on my brain like oil on water.

Chapter 4

Saturday, June 22, 1974

The last time I wore a dress was the day of Mama's funeral, and I never wanted to wear one again. The plaid skirts of my school uniform, worn with a white button-up shirt and a vest or blazer, didn't count.

I classified the seventies as a vast fashion wasteland. When I tried on new styles, they made me a bell-bottomed idiot or the bearer of a pattern and color explosion that might trigger Armageddon. Maybe because Daddy listened to forties music, or maybe because I was simply an outlier, I preferred sporting a hint of the 1940s. Outside of school, I mostly wore boys' rolled-up jeans—which I had to get at the thrift store because they were straight legged and I could roll them easily—and Converse shoes, both of which spent their lives on the bedroom floor instead of folded in the dresser drawer or put away in the closet. On the days my jeans were too wrinkled or smelled funny when I pulled them from the pile, I opted for pedal pushers with bobby socks and loafers, and tried to ignore the insults from the girls at school.

But in the week since Daddy had proposed, dresses appeared in my closet unannounced, hair ribbons materialized on my dresser, and an unseen force cleaned my room. Daddy said Miss Muriel was just helping. *Helping like a bayou gator at a picnic.*

I busied myself that morning dusting the sideboard in the formal dining room with the lemony smell of Pledge and rehearsed The Muriel Argument. Evil stepmothers made you dust every day, kind of like Cinderella, but without the sisters, the fairy godmother, or the pumpkin. Why wasn't it obvious to everyone but me that I did not need an evil stepmother or a Cinderella bridesmaid's dress?

Honey once told me she pretended she was working in a museum while she was doing chores, and that she had to describe the furniture to a tour group. To give myself a distraction from my impending doom that afternoon, I decided to try it.

"And here we have a mahogany table, in use in the Washington household. It's said Martha herself dusted this exact piece. She hated it too. Notice how the chairs have an intricate pattern and tiny carved roses. They are difficult to dust and take an inordinate amount of skill, which makes dusting them seem like a waste of time because the guests are always sitting with their backs against the pattern." I made a show of just how challenging it was by flicking tiny bits of dust from the crevices with my cloth. "They were originally in the collection of Thomas Jefferson. I bet you weren't aware that the Washingtons and Jeffersons shared furniture. It's true. Look it up."

Daddy laughed from the doorway. "Who are you talking to?"

I felt my cheeks flush. "I'm a tour guide in the Thibodeaux Museum. Makes it go by faster. I'm going to Honey's when I'm done." I sprayed the table again and buffed a circle on the dark surface.

"Did you forget about shopping with Miss Muriel to pick out a bridesmaid's dress today?"

I stiffened. The can of furniture polish slipped out of my hand and rolled across the floor, where it stopped at Daddy's feet.

I dashed over to pick it up. "Was that today?" I asked casually.

Daddy tossed me a look and went into the kitchen. I followed him, prepared to plead my case, then waited for the right moment as he sat at our yellow Formica kitchen table, lit a cigarette, and leaned back in the chair.

"Daddy?" I asked. "Can I please go play with Honey instead? I don't want a bridesmaid's dress."

An hour later, Muriel picked me up in her 1965 baby blue Cadillac Sedan de Ville.

Margaret of Thibodaux

"We're going to have so much fun," Muriel said as I slouched in the passenger seat, trying to disappear into the plushy cloth.

Downtown, the buildings were galleried, as in New Orleans, with intricate tendrils of wrought iron reaching through the second stories, holding the galleries up like a waiter holding a tray. The bridal shop was at street level, so Muriel parked in front of the building. She actually clapped her hands as she hopped out of the car. I rolled my eyes.

A young girl, the spitting image of an older lady standing near a mirror in the middle of the room, met us at the door. Next to the mirror-lady stood another exact copy, a few years older than the first. They all had erect posture like books were on their heads, hairstyles that matched Muriel's, and permanent smiles. The ladies seemed to know Muriel as they cheek-kissed hello and congratulated her.

Dipping her chin, she said, "Thank you. You're so kind."

As I imagined a hole in the floor swallowing me up, she added, "I wonder if you could help us find a bridesmaid dress for my . . . for Margaret." She waved her hand in front of me as an introduction, like I was the showcase on *The Price Is Right*.

The youngest shopgirl looked me up and down then came at me with a measuring tape. Before I could protest, she had encircled it beneath my armpits.

"I'm sure we've got the absolutely perfect dress," another said with confidence.

The first dress was awful: flamingo pink and fluffy with tulle underneath. Number two wasn't any better: bubble-gum pink with a bodice so tight I couldn't take a full breath. The only good thing about pink was that I tasted chocolate if I concentrated on it. (Colors had taste for me, though I never told anyone. I didn't need something else to make me stand out from normal folks.) One by one, ever more ridiculous dresses in ever more hideous shades of pink were brought for me to try on.

As I paraded around the shop, Muriel played the part of a lovely Southern woman who loved her soon-to-be husband's only child. Her bouffant hairdo was arrayed on her head like a helmet, and her fake smile never diminished as she batted her eyelashes, "Bat, two, three, bat, two, three," like her eyes were waltzing or something, cooing "Ooooh, this one's pretty" at each dress. She smelled like tuberoses after the rain, but that one redeeming quality could not overcome her other deficiencies.

When I came out of the dressing room for the seventh time, it was in yet another flouncy, girly, tea-length pink abomination, accompanied by my black Chuck Taylors, white gloves, and a pout any four-year-old would envy. The color clashed with my Acadian dark hair and pale skin, making me look like Popeye's girlfriend Olive Oyl in a tutu. Surely, this was not the dress. None of them were the dress. There wasn't a dress.

"What do you think?" Muriel's voice was soft and irritating.

"Too pink," I said. "Too—just—no."

"Oh, but you look so pretty in it. We'll take it!" Muriel said, smiling at me.

I knew better than to be rude and ask her what about the word "no" she didn't understand. So I trudged into the dressing room and changed back into my dignified clothes.

When I came out, the salesgirl handed me the dress, now sheathed with a plastic bag. On the way home, I held The Abomination in my lap as Muriel drove and chirped like a happy little bird.

"The sky sure is pretty." It was.

"And the dress is perfect." It wasn't.

When she pulled up to our curb, Daddy ran out to kiss her through the driver's window. I made it into the house unnoticed and stood in the foyer with the dress hanging over my arm, timing Daddy on my watch. Nine full minutes.

He strolled in and pointed to the cheap plastic bag. "How'd it go?"

"I'll look like a bottle of Pepto Bismol threw up on me."

"Well, make sure you put it up," he said without a speck of sympathy. "Don't throw it on the floor like you do with all your other clothes."

"Yes, sir."

In my room, I took the dress out of the bag and held it up to myself in my full-length mirror. Why Daddy thought a teenage girl needed such a thing bewildered me. Did I really need to see myself from top to bottom? Or what I was going to look like in the near future on Daddy and Muriel's wedding day? There would never be a time I liked this dress, or more specifically, me in it.

I slid the plastic bag back over it and hung it in my closet, way in the back so I didn't have to paw through it every day to get to real clothes. Daddy may have forced me to accept this dress as a gift from Muriel, but I had made up my mind: I would never, ever wear it.

I pouted in my room for most of the afternoon, but when my stomach growled, I decided I'd rather confront Daddy than go hungry. Confrontation was my least-liked action on any level. I'd already lost the battle of shopping for the dress, and I didn't know how many more skirmishes lay ahead. Mama's things were my next campaign, and supper was the perfect time to do my signature poking and prodding.

I loped downstairs to the scent of shrimp cooking in butter, another of Daddy's simple dishes he made in the cast-iron skillet, augmented by a wedge of iceberg lettuce and cherry tomatoes for a salad. I loved how the smell of the shrimp in butter stayed in the air for hours, reminding me of Mama's cooking. Hers was much more complex and time-consuming than Daddy's, but his was as tasty most of the time.

Daddy said a Catholic-Protestant version of grace, which was different each time, with thanks and praise for the main components and an offhand request for someone's health thrown in. Tonight, he asked for Colonel Sanders—an Army man, not the chicken guy—to get the operation he needed. He almost always forgot to say "Amen," so I wasn't sure he'd finished the prayer. When I peeked at him, he was reaching for his fork, so I said "Amen" because I couldn't leave it unsaid.

"Amen," he echoed.

I picked up my wedge of lettuce and bit into it like a sandwich. The crunch was pleasing. "What operation does Colonel Sanders need?" I remembered him, though I hadn't seen him in a year or so.

"It's not any of your concern."

"But if you're asking me to pray for him, shouldn't I know what I'm praying for?"

"No. God'll know." He popped a shrimp into his mouth. "Why don't you come to church with Miss Muriel and me tomorrow? You'd like St. John's. Episcopal is a lot like Catholic."

When I didn't say anything, he added, "You don't have to decide now. Service is at four o'clock if you want to go."

I swirled the shrimp on my plate. "How do you know if God answers your prayers? What's the endpoint?"

"The endpoint?"

"When we do science experiments, there's a point when your hypothesis is either confirmed or denied, the endpoint. What's the endpoint for your Colonel Sanders prayer?"

"I guess he gets his operation." Daddy continued eating at his usual fast pace, left over from being in the Army, and didn't look up from his food. Watergate reporters droned from the living room.

"But what if he gets the operation and still dies?"

"Margaret Louise!" Daddy slammed his hand flat on the

table. He paused then took a deep breath. "Please leave it alone. I'm too tired to have an existential conversation tonight."

"Fine." I swerved to a new topic, away from Daddy's frustration. "Miss Muriel sure likes pink."

He brightened at my apparent compliment. "Yes, she does. And she's so pretty in it."

"Nothing in this house is going to turn pink," I said. It was a statement, not a question. "It can stay just like it is."

"Everything changes, Margaret. You can't move into a new home and not bring anything of yours with you. I expect you'll accept anything she wants to change. And since when do you tell me how things are going to be in this house?"

I studied my fingernails, pink polish chipped at the edges.

"Is 'accept anything' going to be a new rule too?"

I could never tell if Daddy would react to my sass by ignoring me, getting mad, or laughing. It's what kept me doing it, the thrill of the unknown, but also to test him.

"Keep it up, and I'll add more. How about you have to wear dresses?"

My eyes grew wide. "No fair. That pink thing I'm supposed to wear in the wedding counts for a hundred dress wearings."

He missed the "supposed to" and drove on. "How about you have to buy Miss Muriel something nice as a wedding gift—with your own money. That could be a rule."

"Sounds more like a punishment. You don't want me to associate gift-giving with punishment, do you?"

He thought for a moment. "No, that would be bad."

I crossed my arms in momentary triumph. "I've got a rule."

Daddy didn't give me verbal permission to proceed, but I did anyway.

"I'm allowed to have Mama's things in my room. They're mine now."

"What things, Pea?"

"Her rosary, her gloves, pictures, whatever I can find that was hers. Shouldn't I be allowed to have them with my things since you don't want them anymore?"

Daddy didn't wince, just stared past me. I'd meant to cut him, to hurt him. But now as I re-sheathed my knife, my stomach churned.

"You can have them," he said.

It was a hollow victory. He suddenly didn't seem like himself, and I was sorry—not that I said so. Instead I asked, "Will you help me look for them?"

I hoped my offer of inclusion would shift his mood, but Daddy just picked up his dishes and walked into the kitchen. When he turned on the faucet, I heard his charming baritone, sad and lonely, sing the words of "Amazing Grace."

Chapter 5

Sunday, June 23, 1974

"Gentleman, listen up on how to kiss a lady." Forties radio played from the kitchen counter as I sat down to breakfast. "Step number one—put your fingers under her chin and lift slightly. Step number two—pull her close. Step number three—gaze into her eyes. Step number four—lean in and kiss her gently."

I giggled and said to Daddy, "Did you need someone to tell you the steps of how to kiss a lady?"

Daddy looked up from his paper. "What are you talking about?"

"The radio. The guy just listed the four steps on how to kiss a lady."

"Oh. No, I guess not."

I took a few bites of bacon, savoring the smell and taste of comfort.

"When did you first kiss Mama?"

Daddy set his paper down. His lips moved but no sound came out while he formulated an answer. Then he said, "Fifth grade. I kissed her on the playground the day after my birthday."

"That's very specific. Did you like her for a long time before then, or was it just spontaneous?"

"Why are you asking?"

"Just want to know more. We never talk about her. And we won't be able to when Muriel . . ."

Daddy pursed his lips like he did when something disagreeable came out of my mouth.

"You can leave *Miss* Muriel out of this conversation."

"Fine. But when did you kiss her?"

"None of your business."

"Yeah, I've heard that a lot lately."

After Honey got home from Mass, I knocked on her door, a few sheets of tracing paper between two pieces of cardboard (so they wouldn't get scratched) in one hand, and three yellow roses cut from the bushes on the south side of my house in the other.

Her father answered.

"Hello, Mr. Sinclair. Can Honey play?"

He turned and called up the stairs, "Honey, Margaret's here," then disappeared into his office.

We still called it "going out to play," and the adults accepted our activity as the innocent thing the words implied. Honey came to the door with the sketchpad and pencils she always carried.

"You've got to come with me to the cemetery," I whispered. "I need you."

A garbage man like Daddy—and much older than his lawyer wife—Honey's father kept a tight rein on her. Her older brother David performed in a never-ending parade of incorrigible behavior, and Mr. Sinclair imagined Honey had acting-up tendencies harbored deep in her character too. He needn't have bothered keeping watch on her, though. Honey was the last person on Earth to misbehave.

"Pop," Honey called to her father, "I'm going out to play with Margaret. Be back by supper."

She pulled the door closed, and we dashed around back, then southeast through the neighbor's yards to St. Charles, which ran into Menard Street. From there, it was only a few blocks to the cemetery.

"We need to find—"

Honey quieted me with an index finger to her lips, pointing to the house we were passing and crossing herself. It was Jezebel's. Taking my arm, she hurried me to the next block.

Once we were safely in front of the Pressler's house, Honey released her grip.

"Miss Muriel bought me a bridesmaid's dress yesterday," I said.

"I bet you're so pretty in it. Is it pink?"

"Very. Thank you." I kicked a rock unfortunate enough to be in my way. "It's horrible. You know I don't want to be in the wedding."

"Why not? You're so lucky." Her voice caressed the words. "She's an angel."

I stopped walking. "What? She's no angel. She's . . . she's . . . she is *not* an angel."

Honey shrugged and continued walking. "Why are we going to the cemetery? Didn't your daddy say you couldn't go there?"

"He never took me to visit or lay flowers, so I assumed he didn't want me there. But he never said I couldn't go." It stung to have told an inadvertent lie to Honey.

Honey bent over to pick a dandelion.

"I need to talk to Mama," I said.

Honey blew into the wisps. "Oh, that again. What do you need to talk to her about?"

I watched my feet moving one in front of the other, approaching the place I feared for no good reason.

"Muriel. I don't like her."

Honey sighed. "I don't see why. The whole town likes her. After all, she's a doctor." Honey said "doctor" with the same intonation as she'd said "angel."

We pretended to balance on the sidewalk, as if it fell away to a crevasse below and we would die if we took one errant step. My rolled-up jeans and Chuck Taylors looked exceedingly boyish next to Honey's summer sandals and bare legs.

"What are you working on?" I asked.

"Bird boots. I had this dream last night where birds landed at my feet, and when I put them on like boots, they flew me away." She flashed me the sketchbook. "How come in dreams, things seem logical, but when you wake up, it's so weird?"

I shrugged. "I like weird."

We neared the stone garden. Confederate jasmine along the outer wall perfumed the resting place of Catholic faithful and sinners alike, while crickets' wings beat ninety-four times a minute. The high iron gates yawned open and beckoned us toward crypts that shone bright white, sitting above ground as natural crematoriums, generations old.

It had been six years, two months, and sixteen days, and I'd never been inside to visit the grave. I stopped at the gate and grasped the black fence with locked elbows.

"I'll protect you," Honey said.

We stepped slowly inside and set out to find the spot where Mama lay. The cemetery was enormous, crowded with centuries of the dead, the alabaster crypts blinding me in the midday sun. I imagined how relaxing it would be to lie down on the sacred grass and watch the clouds make shapes across the wondrous blue sky. It would be too morbid for Honey, though.

"I don't know which one is hers," I confessed.

Two aisles of grass spread out east and west of the main aisle. "Why don't I go left and you go right?" said Honey. "Then we'll meet back here and go to the next aisle."

This seemed a reasonable plan.

Margaret of Thibodaux

Lots of Thibodauxs populated the Thibodaux cemetery: Bronson Thibodeaux, Mary Thibodeaux, and even a few with different spellings. The name of the town was originally Thibodeauxville, named after Stanley Thibodaux, although not accurately if they added an "e." It was shortened to Thibodeaux at some point and then corrected to Thibodaux when they dropped the "e," confusing everyone. But it was the true spelling of the man the town was named after, and since I had the "e" in my name, I was related to all the "e" folks.

Honey stopped at the far end of a row. With a sudden, graceful movement, she sat down on the flat green grass. She didn't call out, but I ran over to her.

"Did you find her?" I asked. I made sure not to yell, which wouldn't be proper in a cemetery.

"No," she said, tears falling down her cheeks.

Honey was the type who cried for all kinds of reasons, so I wasn't alarmed.

"Look. It's a mom and a baby who died two days apart in 1945. The mom died of a broken heart. Can you imagine?"

I weighed that loss against my own broken heart. "Yeah, I can."

Honey looked at me funny. "I mean, no, I can't," I corrected. "I don't want to think about that right now. I found lots of Thibodauxs but no Veone."

Honey stood and smoothed her yellow sundress back down into place. Happy clothes looked lovely on her. "Let's keep looking. She's got to be here somewhere."

We continued combing our search grid, but when we got

to the cross in the center aisle, we both stopped. A whole other set of rows, twice as many as we'd covered, spread out in both directions.

"We'll never find her," I lamented.

"Wait!" Honey said. "Didn't you go to your Grandma Betsy's funeral? Would they be in the same place?"

I shook my head. "No idea. We never visited Mama's grave after Grandma's service. Grandma's in the mausoleum near the oak tree."

Honey pointed. "There's the oak. Over there."

"It's a start . . . but I know Mama's not in the mausoleum."

"How can you know that if you don't know where she is?"

"I just know."

"Well, let's look anyway."

I followed Honey to the far east side of the cemetery, where one of the mausoleum buildings rose like a Greek ruin.

Honey said, "I'll go find your grandma and see if your mama is nearby."

"Okay. And I'll look out here."

I surveyed the rows, hoping Daddy had at least put Mama in the prettiest place in the cemetery. All the graves had a covering over them, some with white crosses, some with flat stones. As I made my way to the tree, I ran my hand along the cold marble crypts. When I reached the giant oak, my eyes landed square on a grave in the shade.

It was Mama's.

"She's here! Over here!"

Honey ran to me the minute I yelled.

I placed the roses where Mama's heart should be under the concrete lid. Then I stood, reverent and somber, at her feet.

Honey plopped down on the grass like she did in our living room. "It's nice to meet you, Mrs. Thibodeaux," she said patting the grave. I loved her for that.

I pulled out my tracing paper and centered it on the stone engraving. Honey held the corners down while I penciled in wide strokes until the page revealed words:

Veone Louise Thibodeaux
Beloved
April 4, 1932—April 4, 1968

Only when the engraving appeared on the paper did I realize it said "Beloved" and not "Beloved wife and mother" the way Daddy said it did. It wasn't enough. The marker should have said how we missed her and wanted her back. It should have said she sang to her child and wore the prettiest perfume. It should have said that her voice was soft, but her laugh had an edge, coming from deep down.

Honey turned a teary face to me. "April 4th to April 4th. She died on her birthday?"

I nodded, my throat too tight to answer.

Near the marker was a small flower holder made of painted white concrete. Anywhere else it would be a vase, but here it was a rain catcher. A slip of paper stuck out from under it, weathered from past downpours.

I tilted the holder to release its catch and sat beside Honey on the grass. She read the faded words aloud:

Resplendent days drift slowly by,
adorned by sunsets bathed in bullion-colored lie.
I weep for you, my loss so truly mourned
'neath accolades of moon and stars and sky.

"Wow. Poetry. I didn't know your daddy wrote poems. That's awful sweet."

Honey handed me the note. I turned it over and back, looking for some other writing, but only a rose drawn to the left of the words added to the text. "Honey, this isn't Daddy's handwriting."

"Are you sure? Who else could it be?"

"I have no idea."

Someone I didn't know wrote my mama poetry, which meant someone I didn't know missed her. The writer hadn't signed it, addressed it, or protected it from harm in an envelope.

Honey touched my arm. "This doesn't mean anything bad. I don't think bad about her. Promise."

But Honey's words couldn't protect me from this. One of my tears fell on the poem and spread over it like bayou water.

—⁂—

As we walked home from the cemetery, Honey's chatter washed over me, her words competing with those in my head. When we reached my house, we took the front porch steps two at a time, passed through the parlor, and made our way into the kitchen to make peanut butter and jelly sandwiches.

"And I told him it didn't matter what his aunt said; gravity obeys the laws of physics, not the will of a swami or whatever from India. Don't you think so?" Honey paused. "Margaret?"

My name snapped my reverie and I nodded, not registering what she'd said but giving her the impression I had. Honey went right back to talking as I mixed the peanut butter and jelly in a bowl before I spread it on the bread. Then I poured us both a glass of milk.

The screen door slapped shut, a sound Daddy despised, as we took our makeshift picnic to the backyard grass. It had just been cut yesterday and smelled like summer. Honey set her sketchpad next to me to work on the dream bird boots. As she drew, she said, "I hope they get married soon. I love weddings. You'll be so pretty. Does your dress have lots of lace and a big skirt?"

I stopped mid-bite. "Are you done?"

Honey grew quiet as she feathered a few lines on the edge of the boot. The pencil made scratching noises on the thick drawing paper, reminding me of Mama scratching my back as I fell asleep.

All I could think about as I took great big bites of my sandwich (in contrast to Honey's nibbles in neat little rows) was that Mama was the most wonderful person I'd ever known. It made sense that someone adored her from afar, but was it from afar? I wanted everyone to adore Mama, but now there was another hint that maybe it wasn't earned or warranted—and Mama wasn't here to defend herself, so I would have to do it for her.

"Where's your daddy today?" Honey asked.

"At church until five or so. He asked me if I wanted to come along, but I said no."

Honey stopped sketching and shielded her eyes from the sun. "He's still going to that Episcopal church?"

"Yep."

"But I thought y'all were Catholic."

"We are. We were. Who knows what we are now. Ever since the Church said Mama was going to hell, he didn't want to hear Mass or all the terrible things some people say about her."

Honey nodded sympathetically.

I lay back onto the cushy grass and looked straight up at a cloud shaped like an elephant drifting in from the Gulf.

"You might think it sounds weird, but I feel like I'd betray Mama if I switched to the Episcopal Church."

"I don't know that she'd care much now."

I didn't agree. Generations of Catholic Thibodeauxs lived and died in this part of Louisiana, and Daddy used to say it was expected of old families to provide fodder for gossips and something to pray over for churchgoers. But he didn't say it anymore after Mama died. And I didn't need the whole religion thing, anyway. Honey was so Catholic that it bled over and covered for me too. Plus, Daddy had started out Catholic but had drifted away in his teens because of forces or influences he never discussed, creating the first of many controversies in our family. When he married my Catholic mother, it muddied the societal waters even more.

I sat up and gulped the last of my milk. "Do you believe in ghosts?" I asked.

"Umm. Spooky ghosts or someone-you-know ghosts?"

"Both, I guess."

Honey returned to her sketching, her dark eyebrows knitted together. "No, I've never seen one. And I don't like to be scared."

"I've never seen one either. I hear them, though."

Honey didn't look up. "What do you mean, 'I hear them'?"

Knowing how Honey felt about these kinds of things, I hesitated to finally tell her. Daddy had shut down any talk of what I experienced, so I'd never told Honey or Robert either. But something made me take the chance. I lowered my voice and said, "I hear Mama sometimes."

Honey looked up, wide-eyed. "You do?"

"Mm hm. She comes and sits at the foot of my bed and sings me the lullaby she used to sing to me when I was little." Honey's attention encouraged me. "I hear other voices too sometimes. They tell me silly things."

Honey bit her lip and I worried I'd gone too far.

"Am I crazy?" I asked her.

Relief washed over me when she shook her head. "No, you aren't crazy. I believe you." Then she whispered, "They don't tell you to do anything bad, do they?"

"Oh, no. I was talking to Mrs. Huffman in the store the other day, and a voice said her grandson was visiting for the summer. Danged if a minute later she didn't say her grandson was coming to visit."

"Hmm," Honey said, resting her chin in her hand. "Have you always been able to hear them?"

"Pretty much, yeah."

"Who are they anyway?"

"I don't know for sure. Daddy says I used to have imaginary friends when I was little, talked to them and everything, but I don't remember. I first heard Mama after the funeral. I was lying in bed, staring at the ceiling and trying to cry real quiet so Daddy wouldn't hear me, because he told me to be strong. And I heard her, plain as day, singing her lullaby."

"How do you know it was her?"

"I just know. She sits near my feet. It gets all warm, you know, like it does. She used to sing the song to me at night until I decided I wasn't a baby anymore and told her not to, so she stopped. Then I missed it, but you can't change something back once you've stopped it."

"Hmm," Honey said again. "Do you hear her all the time, whenever you want?"

I pulled a blade of grass and wound it around my finger. "No . . . that's the thing. I'll hear her for days in a row, and then she's gone for a long spell, and I get worried I'll never hear her again. And now I can't help but worry that she won't come back because Muriel is here."

"Oh," said Honey softly.

"That's why I have to learn how to contact her. I thought if I went to the cemetery, I could. But she's not there. I couldn't feel her like I do in my room at night. And now . . . now I found that danged poem."

Honey sat motionless. I'd just told her more than I'd ever told anyone, and now I wondered if I should have. Finally, she said, "I thought you were kidding when you said you wanted to learn how to talk to your mama. You shouldn't mess with that stuff, Margaret."

Skeptical Honey was a swarthy pirate underneath her holy demeanor, balancing the end of the plank so I didn't fall off when I ventured too far. But my heart sank as she returned to her sketchbook. We were back to square one.

Just then, Robert poked his head out his bedroom window. I waved him over and he was there in seconds. Robert never walked anywhere.

"Whatcha doin'?" he asked.

"Drawing," Honey and I said in unison, even though she was the only one actually doing it.

Robert sat down and pulled a small brown paper bag from his pocket. "I got new jawbreakers today. Yours is blue, Margaret, and I got pink for you, Honey."

"Thank you," we said in unison again.

I caught a softness in his voice when he spoke to Honey.

"We still haven't decided what we're doing this summer," he said. "We need a big adventure or something."

"Daddy's marrying Miss Muriel. That's enough adventure for me this year."

Robert looked at Honey, then at me. "We decided that's good, right?"

I scrunched up my face. Robert got the message.

"Nah, that's bad. Real bad." Robert scooted away from me in jest. "So what are you gonna do?"

"She's gonna be in the wedding," Honey said.

Robert winced. "Rough. Do you get to wear your Chucks?"

I reached to slap his arm but missed. "Nope, not gonna be in any wedding."

"I don't get it," Robert said. "She seems harmless."

"'Seems' being the operative word." I crossed my legs and leaned back on my hands. "I wish she would disappear. Or get run over. Or blown up."

Robert winced again, harder this time. "Ow. Harsh. What'd she ever do to you?"

I rocked myself upright. "She buys me dresses and ribbons for my hair. She wants me to dress like a girl."

"Ooh . . . crime of the century," Robert said. "She deserves the death penalty."

"She's always been nice to me," Honey chimed in. "I know you think she's pushing your mama away, but don't you want your daddy to be happy?"

"Happy? Yes. By himself."

Honey put down her pencil. "I don't think that's logistically possible with you living in the same house."

The beat of silence stretched to a breaking point. Robert and Honey exchanged concerned glances, then Robert said, "No offense, but how do you talk to a dead person?"

"I don't know, but I'm gonna find out."

"What about a Ouija board?" Robert offered.

Honey bristled. I added it to the mental list of things to research.

Another awkward silence ensued, which Robert broke by saying, "How about going to the Talking Tree."

Honey put her pencil behind her ear and jumped up. "Great idea!"

The air was pure Louisiana, thick and heavy, carrying the sounds of the bayou as it crept past the town, birds singing in concert with the leaves rustling in the breeze. When we reached the Talking Tree, Honey laid her sketchbook on the grass and we each slid onto a swing, immediately pumping to see who could go the highest.

"I think Jezebel is the one you need," Robert said as he swung past me.

"Don't encourage her," Honey admonished. "Both of you need to let it go."

Too late. The oil and water of the initial idea were no longer separate. Sin be damned, I would enlist the Voodoo Woman as mentor or ally in my pursuit of Mama.

Chapter 6

Monday, June 24, 1974

Jezebel must be adept at spirit contact. I just needed to walk up to her door and ask her to help me talk to my dead mama. Didn't sound crazy to me at all.

A tap on my window sounded like a blue jay pecking at something on the inside sill. When I jumped out of bed and went to open the window, a small pebble sailed up and hit the glass. Robert stood on the walkway below.

"I'll be down in a few minutes," I called out, then closed the window tightly against the warm, damp Gulf air.

When I got downstairs, Robert was standing on the porch, bouncing a tennis ball. He suddenly seemed taller than me. I wondered when that had happened.

"I want you to help me make something," he said before even saying hello.

His long hair was a mess, but since it was curly, it was easier for him to get away with it.

"What is it?"

"Something I looked up how to make in the library."

"Moonshine?" I guessed.

"Nah, I don't have to look that up."

I laughed. "You know how to make moonshine? Daddy says it burns something fierce going down." I tugged on his arm. "Come on, tell me."

"I'm gonna tell you, but we have to be quiet about it. I have the stuff in my garage, but there isn't enough room to mix it. Can we use yours?"

"Sure. Daddy'll be home for lunch around twelve thirty. Can we get it done by then?"

"I think so."

"Wanna get Honey?"

"No. She won't like it." He checked his watch. "It's about seven thirty, so I think we have just enough time to make it and purify it."

"Purify it? Purify what? What are we making?"

"Nitroglycerin."

"Nitroglycerin!"

His big smile and the funny jog of his eyebrows told me this would be fun—a little dangerous, but fun.

I followed Robert to his garage. He handed me a Styrofoam cooler like Daddy kept his beer in when we had picnics, and then an eyedropper. Robert gathered containers and some glass beakers.

"Can you fill the cooler with ice?" he asked as we headed back to my garage.

"Sure." I dashed into the house and pulled four trays from the icebox. After dumping them into the cooler, I filled up the trays with water so Daddy wouldn't wonder why all of his ice was gone.

In the garage, Robert was setting up the glass containers and a measuring cup. "Pull the cooler over here," he said. "We need it close in case it goes bad."

"What do you mean by 'goes bad'?"

"It's nitroglycerine. What do you think?"

"Oh."

Robert searched left and right. "I'll be right back."

He ran out then returned with an enormous book that had Dewey decimals on the spine.

"Need the book. Don't have it memorized. Will you read it for me? The page is marked. Here." He pointed to a scrap of paper sticking out from the top of the heavy manual.

I sat on one of the sturdy workbenches. "'Making Nitroglycerine. In flask set in the ice bath, mix nitric acid with sulfuric acid. Stir with glass thermometer until the mixture is forty degrees.'"

Robert filled a Pyrex lasagna pan with ice and water, then put a glass flask in it.

"Why are you making this?" I asked.

"My uncle uses it to blow stumps out of new fields he clears on the McMasters' sugarcane plantation. Makes it himself. So when you were talking about Miss Muriel getting blown up the other day, I got curious about making it, just in case." He poured the two liquids together in the flask.

"Just in case? Are you crazy? I didn't mean actually blow her up. I was exaggerating."

"Calm down. I'm not making it to blow *her* up. You reminded me I wanted to know *how* to do it. Last summer I made gunpowder. You remember the black line on my driveway? That was the gunpowder. I lit it when you and Honey were off somewhere. Didn't want you to stop me because it was dangerous. I'm careful. See?" Robert stirred the mixture, drawing an "s" shape in the flask.

I nodded mockingly and continued reading. "'Add the glycerin, a very small amount at a time. Tilt the flask at an angle and rotate it like a cement mixer while adding the glycerin a drop at a time with the medicine dropper. Monitor the temperature and keep between forty and forty-five degrees.'"

Robert sucked some glycerin into the dropper, held the flask, and squeezed out a drop. It ran down the inside and disappeared into the acids. "This is awkward. Will you turn the flask for me?"

I hopped off the bench and carefully set the book down as if it was the nitro itself.

"Hold it like this. Here. Now, turn it."

My hands were shaking and the flask was cold, but turning it in the ice slurry was easy.

Robert added a drop. "Watch the temperature. Tell me if it gets above forty-five."

The thermometer stuck out of the flask while it turned, resting at the bottom of the tilt. The mercury rose and fell after each drop.

While Robert concentrated on not blowing us up, my mind drifted to laying out a plan to get Jezebel to help me.

Does the library have a book about voodoo and spirits? I should read about it before I talk to her so I don't appear stupid. If she can help me talk to Mama, maybe I don't need anything else from her. Daddy won't like this at all. But I have to talk to him about Mama. I need to know who wrote the poem too. Would Mama know? Can spirit see everything? Oh, no. Can she see everything?

My arms ached holding the cold flask in the same position and only moving my fingers to turn it. "Are we done?" I asked.

Robert remained in deep concentration. "Almost. What's the temperature?"

I'd forgotten to monitor the flask for a few drops and let out a squeal when I read it. "Forty-nine. What do we do?"

"Keep turning it. I'll wait a bit to add more. You've got to keep an eye on it."

"Sorry. The train derailed."

"Huh?"

"I lost my train of thought. I forgot. Daydreaming."

Robert got annoyed whenever I spit out lists to explain something when one example would do. "I need it to stay closer to forty, okay?"

Pretending I was the lovely assistant, I turned the flask and called out a temperature every fifteen seconds, annoying Robert now for a new reason.

When he finished with the glycerin, the mixture looked like nonfat milk with globs in it.

"Can you read me the next step?"

"'After glycerin is added, remove from ice bath and stir occasionally. The temperature should be kept below fifty degrees. Twenty-five minutes after the last glycerin addition, the reaction is complete.'"

"Okay. Take it out of the ice and set it here on the table." Robert took over and stirred the mixture as he watched the thermometer, then consulted his watch. "It's eight fifteen. Reaction is done at . . ."

"Eight forty," I said before he finished the math.

We perched on the workbench next to the table and swung our feet back and forth, both sitting on our hands.

"Why didn't you want to tell Honey?" I asked.

"I told you. She wouldn't like it. Too dangerous."

"Are you trying to protect her for some reason?"

"No. Yes. She's, well, she's fragile, that's all."

"Honey? Fragile? Are we talking about the same girl? She's not fragile. Sweet, sure. Nice, absolutely. But fragile? Nah."

"Maybe I don't want her in harm's way," Robert conceded.

"Oh, and it's okay if I get blown up?"

"Yep," Robert said.

I took a swipe at him and he dodged just in time, as always.

He checked his watch every few seconds, making the time pass even more slowly. At eight forty, he jumped down and stood over the flask. "Okay, read what's next."

I walked him through all the final purification steps,

which were tedious and took another three full hours. When he was done with the alchemy, he poured the final mixture into an amber vial and screwed the lid on tight.

"All right. Let's see if these few drops will explode," he said.

"What? Blow it up already? We just made it."

"I know. But I don't want to keep it around and get in trouble if it goes off. Let's take it out into the yard. We can throw it. This little bit won't hurt us."

From my back porch, Robert did a windup and threw the vial like a baseball, aiming at a spot near the oak tree in the far right corner of our property. I covered my ears as it landed in the soft, short grass, but there was no explosion, no pop, not even a puff of smoke to signal detonation.

"Hmm. Weird. Let me try again." Robert rushed over and dug through the grass like he was hunting Easter eggs. "Here it is." He held it up, a silly grin on his face, then jogged back.

Before Robert could wind up his next pitch, I asked, "Will Jezebel help me?"

"Dunno. Just seems like talking to your mama and voodoo have some things in common."

"No, they don't. Voodoo is witchcraft. Talking to Mama is . . . reasonable."

"So, reasonable is the opposite of witchcraft?"

"You know what I mean. You've mentioned her twice. I thought you knew something about her."

"Not much. Only that Honey is scared of her, or of voodoo. Same thing." He held up the vial. "Should I throw it again?" He tossed it up and down, catching it in his palm, closer and closer to me as I scooted farther away. Finally, he gave it another hurl. Nothing.

Again. Nothing.

After trying seven times, bolder with each toss—even making it bounce, which is hard to do off grass—nothing happened.

"Shit," he said. He sat hard onto the back porch step. "What are we going to do with it now?"

"I'm afraid."

"It's just a little bit. It won't hurt us if it explodes."

"No, I'm afraid of going to see Jezebel. Afraid of what Daddy or Honey will say."

"Then don't go."

"You're not much help, Robert."

"I know," he said with his best smile, proud of being noncommittal.

I grabbed at his wrist, and when he pulled it away I caught a glimpse of his watch. "Oh geez. It's almost twelve thirty. Daddy will be home soon." I thought quickly. "What about if we hit it with the sledgehammer? Daddy has the anvil set up in the garage. Let's try that."

"Yeah, but it'll break the vial and spill all over if it doesn't explode."

"We can clean it up with paper towels and then burn it."

Robert was game, so we returned to the garage. He pulled the metal chain of the single bare bulb. It swayed back and forth like an admonishing parent shaking his head no. I ignored the image and cleared off the counter where the anvil sat.

Robert pulled the sledgehammer from the pegboard on the wall and sized up the vial. "I'm not sure I'm brave enough to do this," he said, his voice a little shaky. "I didn't think this out. I was sure it would explode when I threw it. I guess we need to purify it more next time."

"There's not gonna be a next time," I grumbled. "I just don't want my daddy finding out and grounding me for six years. I'll have to sit in my room the whole time and everyone will forget about me. The only good thing is I'll miss the wedding."

"Too bad you're not very dramatic." He raised the hammer over his head. "Here goes." Like a railroad man, he brought the hammer down with a mighty swing.

A boom rang in my ears. The hammer's head shot straight up and through the roof. A burning smell surrounded us. I surveyed the space around and above us to make sure no fire crawled across the beams, then we ran out and searched for the hammer head.

As I touched blood trickling down the right side of my neck, I saw Daddy rise from his chair on the back porch, a can of Miller beer in his hand and his hat perched on the table next to him. "Well, I hope that's the last of it," he said through the ringing in my ears.

I turned to Robert wide-eyed and shrugged an apology. We knew Daddy would tell Robert's mom and we'd both be in trouble. I also knew immediately that Jezebel was off the table for a while.

"I'm sorry, Daddy," I squeaked out.

"You and Robert are gonna have to fix the roof this weekend. And I think you know you're grounded. Say goodbye."

I waved at Robert, and he turned toward his house, his shoulders slouched as if punishment were already heaped upon him.

Chapter 7

Friday, June 28, 1974

Daddy sat across from me at the kitchen table, reading the morning paper, a cigarette burning between his fingers while he held his cup. His coffee smelled wonderful. I'd been asking if I could have some, but this morning was not the time to win that prize.

As I picked at my eggs and bacon, arranging them on the plate so they didn't touch, I hummed Mama's lullaby.

"Where did you hear that song?" Daddy asked, flattening the newspaper on the table. His voice had an edge to it I didn't recognize.

"It's the one Mama used to sing."

"I remember. Why are you singing it now?"

I tried to be nonchalant. "She sang it to me last night. My ear hurt, and I heard her singing."

Daddy fiddled with his cigarette, tapping it against the

ashtray to keep it burning long after the ash had whittled to the smallest ember.

"She sang to you? You mean you remembered her singing."

He said the last part as a statement in a way that made me shiver, like when someone walks over your grave, then picked up the paper again and held it up like a shield.

I wasn't ready to stop talking about Mama. I wanted the conversation to start and never end. I wanted there to be a place for her still, even if she was gone.

"Daddy, I heard her. I heard her with my own ears, and it wasn't my imagination."

Daddy snuffed out his cigarette and got up from the table. He grabbed his hat and lunchbox. "Don't blow anything up," he said as he let the screen door slam behind him.

At 10:00 a.m., two men in dirt-stained jumpsuits showed up at the house to fix the hole in the roof of the garage. Daddy relented on his demand that Robert and I fix it over the weekend since rain was coming by afternoon. I wasn't fond of heights, and I'm sure Daddy knew the job required real professionals, so it was for the best.

What took the workers forty minutes would have taken hours for Robert and me. I brought them each a glass of sweet tea when they finished, then they packed up and drove off in their handyman truck just as thunder boomed in the distance. The timing was perfect: the early-morning sun fading into clouds created the perfect backdrop for my long-awaited task.

I climbed the steep, narrow stairs into the attic, which were never my favorite because getting down them again was always frightening. I flipped on the light and surveyed the space. Old furniture. Boxes and boxes of who-knows-what. My baby things in one corner.

I decided to start with the big trunk that held my childhood keepsakes. Finding nothing new, I closed the lid and sat down on it. I scanned the room again. In the far opposite corner, poking out behind a large portrait of my grandparents (that Daddy hated so it lived up here), was a similar trunk I'd never seen before. I stood and approached it like it would open by itself if I got too close.

I scooted the painting over and slowly lifted the lid. Its hinges were smooth, and it opened easily. In the very top was a tray set on hooks. And right there, in the tray, were Mama's things. I touched her pearl necklace, her gold wedding band, her rosary. One of her white gloves missing its mate lay beside a crucifix that used to hang on Mama and Daddy's bedroom wall. Her perfume bottle sat there too, three-quarters empty. Even the rings and the lock of my hair from daddy's nightstand drawer were there. How could he have told me he didn't know where Mama's things were as if he had forgotten? I slipped Mama's wedding ring onto my right pinky. She had the most delicate little fingers, but I didn't inherit those. I got Daddy's chunky hands instead.

In the lower part of the trunk, I found a blue baby blanket.

I hadn't thought ahead to getting back down the stairs with Mama's things, but the blanket seemed like the perfect solution. I carefully loaded the treasures like Santa with his pack and eased my way down the creaky steps.

When I got to my room, I arranged each item on my dresser top. Fine if Daddy no longer wanted her things. They were mine now.

I moved over to my window and watched the rain fall in torrents. With each rumble of thunder, my heart raced, followed by the thrill of lightning exploding in bursts of eerie fingers. Mama and I were both fascinated by things in the sky, but Daddy couldn't have cared less. Weather was the thing you talked about if you didn't know what to say. I couldn't fathom how anyone could think it was boring.

At dinner one night last week, Daddy announced that it was hurricane season, giving me hope that he was coming around to my way of thinking. But the topic I wanted him to come around on even more was Muriel. He sure smiled like an idiot when he talked about her.

As the rain let up, little white butterflies flitted along the grass in the front yard, and I imagined them sipping from water drops on the grass. Mama loved butterflies too, specifically the nondescript white ones that appeared alone. I decided Mama had sent them, coming to say hi in a different way. Or maybe she sent them to tell me she was happy her things were no longer hidden away.

Being grounded was old school, but Daddy's version was brutal. Most of my schoolmates got something taken away, like no sweets or talking on the phone. But because I didn't care about either of those things, Daddy chose banishment. Life would have been so much easier if I'd pretended I loved candy so that when I got in trouble, I'd give up something I didn't actually like. Honey would die if she couldn't have sweets, but no such luck for me. I had to suffer true deprivation. Even when Napoleon was exiled to an island, at least he could go outside.

I opened the window and breathed in the air. The wet concrete and grass had the distinct after-the-rain smell I loved. Just then, I heard the guttural, pitched sound of Honey's brother David approaching in his Mustang. His right hand hung over top of the wheel and his left patted the open window frame. I doubted he smelled the after-rain scent. He only ever thought about himself and which girl liked him.

Just as he and his two ever-present friends passed, he looked up and caught me in the window. I dropped to the floor as my face flushed from anger more than embarrassment. He would misinterpret my stare, and nothing would right the story in his mind. He'd tell his friends too, and they'd all point at me and laugh.

A few minutes later, someone knocked on the door. I had no way of seeing who it was, but everyone answered their door in Thibodaux, so I couldn't pretend not to be home, especially not when I was grounded. Praying it wasn't David, I opened it.

"I brought you a sandwich," Honey said. "Mother said you must be lonely."

I let out a sigh of relief that it wasn't David, but Honey took it as relief from loneliness.

"Thank you." I stepped back to let Honey in but she didn't move.

Instead she said, "I better get home. Mother said we're going shopping for dinner and . . ."

"And what?"

Honey shuffled her foot back and forth on the wooden porch, then took in a breath. "And she's taking me to the Girls Club so I can make some new friends."

"What? Why do you need new friends?"

Honey hesitated again, then parroted her mother's words: "Your current friend blows things up. You need new ones."

My mouth dropped open. I hadn't considered grown-ups might now consider me to be dangerous, even though I wasn't. But Honey's mother was a lawyer and dealt with juvenile delinquents all the time. Exhibit A: David.

A dove landed on the porch railing. "She'll soften up," Honey said, "she always does." Honey patted my arm. When she turned to leave, she noticed the dove and said, "Keep an eye on her," then giggled at her own joke.

"Tell your mother thank you for making me a sandwich. She can't be too mad at me if she feeds me."

Honey giggled again.

As she started down the steps, I added, "I hope you don't make any new friends."

Honey swiveled around and smiled. "Don't worry. I won't."

Chapter 8

Sunday, June 30, 1974

Two days later, still grounded, I opened my journal to make a new entry.

Punctuation and I have a love-hate relationship. I love all those cute little marks that help me express myself, and they hate me by misbehaving and being elusive, never revealing their inner feelings. I get slightly annoyed by this.

For some reason, I've been thinking about the guy in Catcher in the Rye. We read it last year. He thinks everyone, deep down, is bad. I think, deep down, everyone is good, and I'm shocked when they prove they aren't. But I get over it. When his sister asked him to make a list of things he liked, he had a

Margaret of Thibodaux

hard time coming up with anything. I have a long list of things I like:

- green
- strawberries
- fresh-cut grass
- the way sand looks when it's falling through your fingers
- yellow paint
- hamburgers
- Chuck Taylors
- jeans
- PB&J sandwiches
- history
- purple
- a baby's laugh
- skipping
- lightning bugs
- the smell of old books
- storms with lightning and thunder
- the feel of window glass on a cold winter day
- popcorn
- the moon

In The Prophet, Kahlil Gibran says to "let your best be for your friends." I think that is a very nice idea, but what if I need to keep the best parts of me for me? What if I need to use them myself later? Am I being too selfish?

I've decided to wear Mama's gold wedding band on my pinky finger to keep her close to me. Hope Daddy doesn't notice . . . or maybe I hope he does.

Why do great ideas come when you're in the shower and can't write it—

There was a soft knock on the bedroom door. Honey slipped in and closed it behind her before I had a chance to get up. Her mother must have relented on the friendship ban.

"What are you doing here?" I whispered. "You know I'm grounded." My voice cracked from not talking much for days.

"Your daddy's asleep in his recliner downstairs, so I let myself in." Honey beamed with pride and sat on my bed. "I tried to see you yesterday, but he said no visitors, even after I told him that you and Robert making nitroglycerine showed great intellectual curiosity and initiative."

"He clearly didn't buy it."

"No. That's why I had to sneak in."

Grounding was foreign territory for Honey. She was too sweet and well-behaved to even get close.

"How are you doing? Are you bored to death? How's your ear?"

"Ear's better, thanks." Then, with the sarcasm Honey understood and appreciated, I added, "I don't have time to be bored. I'm counting floor tiles."

Honey laughed, then grew serious.

"Is something wrong?"

"You won't believe it," she said, "but someone killed Dr. Martin Luther King's mother this morning. At church. She was playing the organ, and some man just walked in and shot her. Right in the head. It was a black man too."

I put up my hand. Details would cut into my heart like it was my own kin. I'd always tied his family to ours since our loved ones died on the same day.

I also now had another reason not to go to church.

"I'm sure it'll be on the news tonight," said Honey.

"I'm sure." Desperate to change the subject, I said, "Did you make any new friends at Girls Club?"

Honey sneered. "No. They were mean. First, they ignored me, and then when I tried to make friends anyway, one of them shoved me. Can you believe it? Put her hands right on my chest and pushed so hard I fell on my butt."

"How could anyone be mean to you? Do they go to our school?"

"I don't think so. Never saw any of them before. I told Mother I'm not going back and that you and I would be friends whether she liked it or not."

"What did she say?"

"When I showed her the dirt on the back of my dress, she said, 'Battery,' which made me think she was having a stroke or something. Then she said, 'When someone touches you to hurt you, that's battery. It's a crime.' I had to talk her down from going all lawyer on the Girls Club."

"Is that when she decided to let us be friends again?"

"Not exactly," Honey said with a pitch to her voice. "She actually didn't mention you. I think she's going to see how it goes. But since you aren't a delinquent, we'll be just fine."

"Thanks . . . I guess."

Honey traced the pattern of my quilt with her finger. "I tried to see Robert, but his mama is still so mad at him she may never let him out."

"I hope *I* get out."

"Why'd you make the nitroglycerine?" Honey didn't beat around the bush.

"It sounded fun at the time."

"You could have been killed. Robert, too. I would have been all alone."

"I'm sorry." I really was.

I looked toward my window. It was misting rain, giving the outside world an eeriness to it, even at high noon.

"Hey," Honey said tentatively, "I was wondering . . . can I see the poem again?"

"Oh. Sure." I padded to the dresser and slid open the top drawer. I sifted through my socks and pulled the poem from the right front corner. I handed it to Honey as if it was an ancient piece of paper ready to turn to dust.

Honey studied it for a long time. She turned it over, held it up to the cloud-filtered light, and tested the weight of the paper between her fingers. Then she handed it back to me as I had handed it to her.

"Well?" I asked.

"I got nothing. I need to think about it some more."

A look crossed my face that made Honey knit her brow. I took in a breath. "I found Mama's things in the attic on Friday. Just before you came over and brought the sandwich."

"You did? Why didn't you tell me?"

"Because you had to go. You weren't supposed to be friends with me anymore, remember?"

"You know that was never going to happen."

I shrugged.

"Why did your daddy put her things in the attic?"

"I don't know." I squirmed uncomfortably. "Why do we wear white gloves when we go to church or get dressed up?"

Honey tipped her head. "Hmm. I've never thought about it. We just do. Why?"

"When Mama died, everyone wore white gloves, like they do, and The Fish covered their mouths with them after the burial when they talked about Mama. I thought they were telling secrets. Then I heard Mrs. Browner say Mama was going to hell."

"Who are 'The Fish'?"

"Do you think Mama had a secret?"

Honey bit her lip. "Uh, well, I don't think so?" She said it as a question not a statement.

"What about Muriel? Do you think she has a secret?"

"I don't know. I guess it depends on the degree of the

secret. Everyone has something no one else knows, like how many times they go to the bathroom in a day. But just because no one else knows and it's technically a secret, it doesn't mean it's anything worth knowing."

As usual, until Honey dissected the language, I didn't see it clearly. It was one of the best things about being friends with her.

"I guess, but I don't understand what happened and why everything around Mama is such a big secret. I'm older now. There's nothing I wouldn't understand. But Daddy won't talk about her. And who else can I ask? You didn't know her, and I'm certainly not going to ask The Fish.

"Don't you have family on your mama's side you can ask?"

"We haven't had contact with any of them since she died."

"Why?"

"I don't know."

"Weird. I'd hate to not know my aunts and uncles and cousins."

"Mama had a small family. Both her parents had died, but she had two sisters and a crazy Aunt Margaret."

Honey giggled.

"I know. Figures the crazy aunt has my name." I rolled my eyes. "Mama's sisters live near Mobile, or at least they did, so maybe it's a distance thing?"

It suddenly dawned on me how strange it was that no one on Mama's side of the family had ever made an effort to see me after Mama's death.

"Maybe."

"I wouldn't even know them if I saw them on the street."

Honey played with the hem of her dress. "You've sure had a lot of time to think, haven't you?"

"Too much."

"When are you done being grounded?"

"Three more weeks, but I'm going to lobby for two weeks total for good behavior. Even then, I won't be out until after the Fourth of July."

"Oh, so no parade or fireworks?"

"Nope."

"Too bad. Probably not Robert, either. My folks said I could go with David and his friends."

"That's risky."

Honey laughed because it was true, then stood up. "I'd better get going. I don't want to have to escape out your window if your daddy wakes up. Then you'll really be in trouble." She tiptoed to my door. "Hey, come to Mass with me Sunday."

I weighed being grounded in my room with going to church. Oddly, the scale tipped wildly toward church.

"Okay, I'll ask. Can't imagine he'd say no to that. He's pretty annoyed with me, though. You should have seen the garage roof. Hole right through it. He said he was mostly disappointed in me, that he couldn't trust me anymore."

"Oh, it was just a minor lapse in judgment. He'll get over it. I hope."

"Me too." Then I added, "Do you still trust me?"

"Implicitly."

"Should I talk to your mother? About us being friends still?"

"I'd steer clear of her for a while. David is giving her fits right now. Just don't do anything like that again, okay?"

I said "Okay," but even for Honey, I was hesitant to give up my rights to misbehave if the situation warranted it.

Chapter 9

Monday, July 8, 1974

"Daddy," I pleaded at breakfast that next day, "may I please be off grounding? I've done all my chores and learned my lesson."

"Oh? What lesson did you learn?"

It was too early on a Monday morning for a precise defense of this argument, so I settled for the obvious. "Well, for sure not to make nitroglycerine again."

"Yes, what else?"

Daddy had let me out the day before to go to Mass with Honey. Big mistake. The visiting priest came barefoot, played the guitar, and sang "Let It Be." I know I'm not the best Catholic, but what in the holy hell was that?

"Not to go to church just to get out of the house, especially if Father Something or Other is saying Mass."

Daddy laughed. He agreed with me on that one, so I won

my plea for leniency on general grounds. I'd lost two whole weeks of my life and vowed to myself I wouldn't do anything to risk time again. It was too precious.

"I'll want you to tell me where you're going and what you're doing for the rest of the summer," Daddy said.

I nodded acceptance of the terms of my parole, though Daddy's wary eye wasn't something I anticipated or liked. I hated scrutiny and wondered how Honey tolerated it from her folks without ever complaining.

Robert's doorstep was freshly swept and washed, forbidding dirty shoes. Mrs. Pennington answered on the first knock.

"Can Robert come out to play?" I asked with my most adorable smile.

"No."

The door slammed in my face. I got the distinct message Robert's mama regretted her acquiescence to "one more kid summer." She was strict in the way single mothers can be, but I didn't blame her—Robert was a handful, but at least his type of naughty was mischief and not malice. I hoped Mrs. Pennington let him come out before we graduated high school.

I glanced up toward his window and saw his forlorn face looking down at me. A feeble wave was all he could muster. I waved back.

"We're going to the Talking Tree if you can make it!" I said a little too loudly.

His mama parted the curtains and glared at me, and I bounded off to retrieve Honey.

We walked the several blocks to the bayou, chatting about the usual stuff, thankfully avoiding the subject of Muriel, the dress, and the wedding. When we reached the swing set, we jumped into adjacent swings and pumped as high as we could go, our hair whipping back and forth while we taunted gravity. Robert's empty swing hung still and sullen without his rambunctious laugh.

The higher we flew, the more gigantic beads of sweat lined my forehead until they became a stream. I used to wonder why I got pretty handkerchiefs each Christmas when I was little. When I got older, I realized they kept your face from drowning. At church, The Fish reached into their tops and drew out crumpled lace hankies, dried their necks and faces, then tucked them back into their bosoms. I swore I would never keep mine there. They were useful, though, so I started stealing Daddy's plain white ones and tucking them into my back jeans pocket. It counted as another reason not to wear dresses until I realized Honey had pockets in all of hers just for hankies.

At the same time I whipped my simple one out, Honey reached for her frilly, girly version. After a few swipes, we jumped from the swings and settled on the grass under the shade of the oak, each of us picking dandelions into fuzzy little bouquets.

"I've been thinking about the poem," Honey said. "If someone loved your mama besides your Daddy, it could have been from afar, right? I asked Pop—"

I bolted upright. "You did what?"

"Touchy. I just asked Pop if he ever wrote poetry to my mother."

"And?" I crossed my arms, embarrassed that I'd jumped to a conclusion.

"He laughed and said no. I asked him if he ever wrote poetry at all, and he said the only person he knew who wrote poetry was old man Merriweather."

"You think he wrote Mama poetry?"

Honey laughed. "Not likely."

I pictured the old man leering at Mama and closed my eyes to make it stop. "So, that doesn't clear anything up."

"Well," Honey reasoned, "it was sitting under the vase on her grave, right? Maybe it was on another grave, or in the street, or in the grass, and someone picked it up and decided your mama's grave was where it belonged."

"Thank you."

"For what?"

"For trying to find a way for it to be an accident instead of a mystery."

"I don't want it to be a mystery," Honey said.

"Me neither, but that's what it is. I just hope it's not unsolvable."

I lay back in the afternoon heat, catching the breath of a breeze. Honey mirrored me.

"I just want people to remember her like I do."

Honey grew quiet. "Margaret?"

"Yeah?"

"How did she . . . die?"

I stared up at the cottony puffs dotting the sky. Honey had been too polite to ever ask.

"I'm sorry to ask now, but maybe you can find an answer to the poem by telling me."

I brought the dandelions to my face and gently blew their seeds into the air.

"Daddy said there were sleeping pills on her bedside table," I said quietly. "The bottle was on its side and half empty. She was dead when he found her. I came home from school not long after. Daddy sent me to Grandma Betsy's house right away."

"Was it an accident?" Honey asked. "Some folks say she did it on purpose."

"I know. But yeah, I'm pretty sure it was an accident. I don't even know why she had the pills in the first place. Daddy was heartbroken. Me too." I picked a blade of grass and tore it lengthwise.

"Is that why you don't go to church anymore?"

"Well, the Church says that if you kill yourself, you'll go straight to hell. I don't believe it. I feel her and hear her. How can she be in hell?"

Honey didn't answer. She was about as Catholic as a girl could be outside of a convent.

"Do you think she's in hell?" I asked.

"Of course not. It was an accident. I'm sure of it."

"The Fish gossip about her and say she did it on purpose. They're all practically deaf and don't realize they're almost shouting when they think they're whispering to each other."

Honey touched my arm. "I'm sorry. I don't know what to tell you."

"You don't have to tell me anything. Just listening is fine. It's not fair is all. I want to protect her . . . I still want her advice." I waited a beat. "That's why I'm going to try to find some way to talk to her."

Honey sat up. "I really don't think you should do that, Margaret."

"I'm going to the library tomorrow to find a book on how to contact spirits."

Honey crossed her arms and shook her head. "I won't help you. I don't like it one bit."

"Well, then, I'll find someone who will." I got up and left Honey sitting on the grass. My eyes welled up with tears as I walked away.

Chapter 10

Tuesday, July 9, 1974

The trip to the library was laden with nerves. Mrs. Right, the librarian, knew Daddy, and she was known to let parents in on the searches of their children if she thought they should know. Pregnancy, birth control, sex—those were the topics she'd rat on you about. I wasn't sure whether she thought spirits were reportable. Luckily, I sleuthed out a book on my own that had an overview of Ouija, crystals, voodoo, and meditation. When I checked it out, I was sure Mrs. Right would read the title. She didn't. After she handed it to me, I scurried out before I could run into any of my classmates.

No one was home when I got there, but still I ran up to my room and locked the door. I flipped the book open and skimmed the interior with excitement, but the gist that all spirit contact was evil defeated me. It did include a chapter on the methods of contact, but of course they were all evil too and therefore lacked instruction. I left the book on my bed and plodded downstairs to get a snack.

A ripe, fat watermelon sat on the sideboard. I brought it to the kitchen and hacked out a big slice. Licking the juice, I took it outside to the front porch steps—the perfect place for spitting seeds. After aiming a few for distance, I began aiming them at Muriel. The target was her face, smack where a big crack ran through the concrete. After several hits and only a few near misses, Honey came up the walk and saved me from myself.

"Want to draw?" she asked. "I brought some chalk."

"Sure. What's the subject today? You pick."

"How about angels? I got a whole bunch of white. Angels make me happy," Honey said with a dreamy smile.

We laid the chalk on the grass, staked out two squares on the long walk, and drew a line halfway to the house to divide it into two canvases. I wasn't as good at drawing as Honey. She made great sweeping strokes while I studied the space first, then slowly sketched the initial lines. Only a distant dog bark and the occasional honking horn pierced our silence.

When Honey finished, she said, "I made my angel like Miss Muriel."

"What? How could you draw Muriel as an angel? Don't you think you might offend a real angel, like Mama?"

Honey brought her chalked-up hand to her mouth. "Oh, I'm sorry. I didn't even think . . . I didn't mean anything by it. I think you're so lucky. Now you have one in heaven and one here on Earth."

"I don't need one here," I snapped, then softened. "But your drawing is pretty." It looked like Muriel. My angel had turned out more like a ghost with dark eyes, a blurry outline, and an ox tail.

I resumed drawing. "Do you think the Ouija board works?"

Honey crossed herself in a deliberate, swift motion. "Mother would kill me if she knew we talked about that. What's wrong with you?"

"I didn't mean if you'd actually *tried* it. I meant, you know, could it be possible?"

Honey glared at me, her usual sublime smile gone in an instant. "I don't want to talk about it, Margaret Louise."

She returned to her drawing, adding in some contrast for her angel's face, and using blue, green, and white to make the unique shade of Muriel's eyes.

"The Johnsons got a new poodle," she said in an attempt to change the subject. "He's a toe-licker."

I didn't want to talk about anything else.

The air around us cooled as clouds rolled in off the Gulf. The usual summer thunderstorm would soon follow.

Honey was distant as she said, "I guess I'd better pack up."

I helped her pick up the chalk and said goodbye, then watched her flit home, skipping and singing.

My library book was a huge disappointment, but it did have a section on Ouija. I went up to my room and read about how it attracted the base-level spirits and that you had to be careful—whatever that meant. The section on crystals was mildly interesting, but I decided that access to crystals would come through Jezebel whenever I got the guts to approach her house. I skipped to the chapter on meditation to find that most of it made little sense. Still, after I read it, I closed my eyes and tried to focus on my breathing, in and out, in and out. I woke up to the slam of a car door and the sun low in the sky.

When he was hungry and supper wasn't ready, Daddy was a bear. I hurried downstairs and pulled a can of chili from the cupboard, rolls from the bread box, and green beans from the icebox just as Daddy came into the kitchen. He said nothing about dinner being late, just grabbed a beer and a tray and planted himself in front of the TV for the latest update on Watergate.

He thanked me when I served him supper, but he was silent otherwise. The meditation section of the book talked about "resistance" and how it was a bad thing. That's what I felt from Daddy, like he was building a stone wall right in front of me.

Though the rain hadn't started, thunder rumbled through the screen door. While I ran water for the dishes, Daddy said from the TV room, "I saw the drawings on the sidewalk. One looks like Miss Muriel."

"Honey drew it. She's pretty talented."

"I'm glad you gravitated toward a sedate activity," he teased.

I smiled. At least he was teasing me and didn't still have me locked away like Robert.

The phone rang, unusual for seven o'clock. I dried my hands and answered it.

"Thibodaux residence, Margaret speaking."

It was Honey's second cousin, Ginger. I took the phone to the end of the kitchen so Daddy couldn't hear and thanked her for returning my call, then lowered my voice for good measure. "Hey, remember a few months ago when you were talking in school about having a Ouija board you hid from your mother?"

"Yes, why?"

"May I borrow it?"

"Sure. I don't see why not."

We agreed on a meeting time the next day, then I hung up the phone and pretend-clapped my hands as I dashed back to the sink to finish the dishes.

"Margaret?" Daddy called.

"Yes, sir?"

"Who was on the phone?"

"Ginger. Honey's cousin. She wanted to know if we wanted to buy some Girl Scout cookies."

"Oh. Did you get some Thin Mints?"

"Yes, sir. Two boxes."

It was true, what I said. Part of it. I apologized to Mama for lying as I finished washing the chili pot, wondering who might have a box or two of Thin Mints they'd be willing to part with for a good cause.

Chapter 11

Friday, July 12, 1974

On Wednesday, I rode my bike to pick up the Ouija board from Ginger, who swore me to secrecy on the penalty of death if her mother found out she had it. The book said you needed at least three people to make it work, and she agreed to be one of the three. There was no one else I trusted except Robert, but he was still grounded, so I decided to ask Honey to join us. I knew she'd refuse and throw a fit, but the instruction book said that having a skeptic present made the results more valid. I figured if I could get her to participate just this once, it was better to have her know and disapprove than to wonder and make things up.

I set the date and time for the "game" on Friday morning at my house. Honey had been expectedly noncommittal when I asked her, so I was surprised to find her standing on the porch with her cousin when I opened the door on the appointed morning of the experiment.

Honey's arms were firmly crossed over her red gingham dress. As the designated skeptic, she agreed to be present and lend her fingers, but not to participate in any other way. She had already covered the event with a dozen Hail Marys and asked forgiveness for the sacrilegious part she was playing. She'd also repeatedly expressed her displeasure at my wanton disregard of her opinion that all the methods under consideration to contact my mama were tools of the devil.

"Why can't you pray for answers?" she pleaded one last time as we climbed the stairs to my room. "It's so much simpler."

"Annabelle Jane, if you're negative the entire time I'm trying to talk to Mama, she won't come. She never met you, and you'll scare her away."

Honey huffed as the three of us sat on the floor of my room. I'd refused to open the box alone, even though I'd had it at my house for two days. We placed the board on the shiny wood parquet and stared at it as if it was a *Playboy* magazine—forbidden and dangerous but promising knowledge, or something like it.

"That's it?" I said. "It's a bunch of letters and numbers."

"There's more," Ginger said, pulling out the table-looking thing with a plastic window and a pointer.

I hadn't expected a ghost to fly out of the box or anything, but still it seemed anticlimactic.

I had already closed the curtains to dim my room of the morning light. Ginger read us the instructions.

"'Do not allow the planchette'—it's called a planchette—'to count down through the numbers or backwards through the alphabet.'"

"How are we supposed to stop it?" I asked.

"You'll see when we start." She continued, "'Always place a silver coin on the board before playing.' Shoot. I forgot about the silver coin. Guess I missed it before."

"I have one," I offered. "Well, I know where one is anyway. Be right back." I ran downstairs to the living room and opened the case where Daddy kept his coin collection. I picked one labeled "Gordian III" and rushed back up with the prize.

"Here. We can use this." I handed it to Ginger, who placed the coin in the upper left corner near the sun, then read more from the small booklet. "'Never mention God. The entities are evil and will disappear at the mention of God's name. Always say goodbye when the session ends.'"

I was certain the mention of evil predicted a cross from Honey. She was less frantic about it this time, but still she made one, slow and deliberate.

With the board in the center of our compact circle, we put our fingertips on the pointer.

Ginger said, "We are relaxed. The spirits may make contact."

After several seconds, Honey mysteriously forgot she wasn't participating and asked, "Are any spirits here?"

The pointer remained still as six fingers waited for direction.

Honey added, "Is Mrs. Thibodeaux here? Do you like Miss Muriel?"

"Honey!" I squirmed.

The pointer moved, and we eyed each other, convinced one of us had pushed it. We chanted the letters as the pointer stopped over each of them.

"D - O - N - O - T."

"Donot?" Ginger said. "What's a donot? Is it like a donut?"

"It's 'do not,'" Honey said, "not donot."

"Oh," Ginger and I said in unison.

The pointer moved again. "L - I - K - E."

"Do not like," I repeated, nodding in agreement. "Of course Mama doesn't like her. But now what do I do? We're supposed to go to dinner at Miss Muriel's house tomorrow night."

The pointer continued to move, making furious arcs over the letters as we struggled to keep our fingers on the flimsy plastic.

"D - O - N - T - G - O," we chanted together.

All three of us removed our fingers at the last letter.

"Don't go," Ginger said, a timbre of fear in her voice. "Margaret, you can't go. It's a warning."

"This is a bunch of hooey," Honey said. "Would your mama scare you?" She placed her fingers back on the planchette, and Ginger and I followed her lead. It moved and displayed the letters through the tiny window before swiping toward the next.

"P - O - E - M."

My heart dropped to the floor and Honey gasped, but we kept our fingers steady. "Yes, we found a poem. What do we need to know about the poem?" Honey asked.

"M - O - R - E."

"More what?" I asked, desperate for answers that made sense. "More of the same poem?"

We sat with hands outstretched and fingers held in lightest touch, but the pointer didn't move again.

"The session's over," Ginger announced.

We lifted our fingers and each said goodbye, eager to end things according to the rules and not risk evil spirits' anger.

We stared at the board, then at each other. Honey scooted away from it first.

Since the board was hers, Ginger started putting the pieces in the box. She handed me Daddy's silver coin and I put it in my pocket.

"Want to go to my house to—"

Before Honey could finish, Ginger blurted out, "Sure!"

They both looked at me with raised eyebrows.

"No," I said. "I need to think about this."

"Well, you go right ahead." Honey looked pointedly at Ginger then at me. "I don't want anything more to do with it. Ever."

I exhaled with relief when the board left my house under Ginger's arm.

I grabbed a hankie from my dresser and my bottle of holy water, then poured a small puddle onto the floor where the board had been. The water spread over the wood while I chased it with the thin white cloth, wiping away all remnants of its presence.

When I finished cleansing the floor, I considered the event. On my right fingers, I ticked off the reasons it was real, on my left, the reasons it could be bullshit.

Honey wouldn't move it. She wasn't deceitful. Right finger up.

Ginger didn't know about the poem. Right finger up.

The pointer moved out from under my fingers more than once. Right finger up.

The answer from Mama was logical but didn't feel real. Left finger up.

Warning from spirit to not go to Muriel's for dinner. Left and right finger up—too soon to tell on that one.

Prediction of another poem—couldn't analyze that yet.

Four real fingers versus two bullshit fingers. And more questions than answers.

I opened my window to let the outside world finish purifying my room and vowed to never get near a Ouija board again.

Chapter 12

Saturday, July 13, 1974

That next morning, Honey and I wandered into the cemetery. Neither of us admitted to going there on purpose, but curiosity made it unbearable to walk by the crypts without going in. The Ouija board had said "poem" and "more," which by themselves meant nothing, but since we had already found one poem, it seemed like a clue.

"Let's go to Mama's grave," I said, making it official.

When her site came into view, I stopped dead in my tracks. "I can't do it."

Honey grabbed my arm as I turned around. "Margaret. Stop. We're here. Let's look. Maybe it's nothing."

We tiptoed toward the grave as if a false move would set off a landmine. As we got closer, a fresh white paper stuck out from under the concrete vase. With trembling hands, I stooped to pick it up and read it aloud.

We have one place left where
No one knows how sensitive we are
To the rejection of being left

"That's not poetry." I read it aloud again, but it still didn't make much sense. "What does it mean? It was definitely left here. Makes it seem like the first one was intentional too."

Honey didn't reply at first. She took the paper and examined it like the proper clue it was.

"Is this the same handwriting?"

"I think so. The other one's in my room. I can compare it when we go home." I took the paper back from Honey. "Let's figure this out."

We huddled over it. After reading it aloud again, I said, "I think the "one place left" means home, or is it a person?"

Honey shrugged. "Could be."

"I don't get who he's trying to message. Me? Mama? Daddy? Seems inefficient to leave notes at a grave. What if no one ever found them? Have they been here all along?" I shook my head back and forth. "Arrrggh . . . I have so many questions!" I stared at the words for so long that they became nonsense. Mama would have the answers, but the Ouija board scared me, so there must be another way.

"I need to talk to Daddy," I announced.

"I thought you wanted to leave your daddy out of it?"

"I do. I did. But maybe he knows something he'd be willing to tell me."

Honey made a face of doubt. "Good luck with getting something from him."

When I got home, the Watergate hearings blared from the TV. Daddy didn't look up when I entered the room. He was focused on the magnifying glass in his hand, peering at a silver coin. I was relieved I'd put the Gordian back last night before he noticed it was missing.

"Daddy?"

"Huh?"

"Did you know humans and armadillos are the only two animals that can get leprosy?"

Still concentrating on his coin, he said, "And where did you find that fascinating bit of information?"

"The library. I was looking for the lwa, you know, spirits, and I found a book on leprosy. They talk about it in the Bible all the time. Guess they don't have armadillos in Jerusalem. Someone dog-eared the page."

The Vodou chapter (I'd learned voodoo was not the right word) said the lwa were the dominant spirits of the religion. I thought the word would get Daddy's attention, but all he said was, "Hmm."

I could see subtlety wasn't going to cut it.

"Daddy, what if I died?"

Without missing a beat, he said. "I'd be sad."

"Would you visit me?"

He still didn't look up. "Can't visit the dead, Margaret."

I pushed on the wall. He held it in place. Honey was right. It was going to be harder to talk to him about Mama than to contact Mama herself.

"Make sure you're ready to go by six. And wear one of those new hair ribbons Miss Muriel bought for you."

"Yes, sir."

I gave in by word, but I wouldn't make it easy on him. Not by a long shot.

"Come on, Margaret!" Daddy called from the porch. "We have to go."

I pictured him slapping his hat against his leg as I stood in my room, dressed and ready, with one last, desperate idea to get out of going to Muriel's house for supper.

I ran in place to raise my heart beat and flush my cheeks with heat, waited until the second yell, then hurried down the stairs and out the door.

"I think I have pneumonia."

"You don't have pneumonia. Get in the car."

"Maybe I have leprosy."

"Margaret Louise, you do not have leprosy. Get in the car, please."

I remained unmoving on the porch, as if I would fall off a cliff if I stepped toward our Dodge Dart.

"What's the matter with you today?"

It was unnatural to disobey him, but the conviction I had about not going to Muriel's won the pull inside me. "I don't want to go," I whispered, my head hanging like a shamed hound.

Daddy sighed "Why not?"

"Mama wouldn't like it."

Tension sprang up between us. He stared down at his hat and ran his thumb over the brim. I couldn't tell if he was mad or shocked.

"Get in the car," he said.

It was silly to assume I could resist and he'd give in. Daddy wouldn't make it that easy. And now I had to go where Mama warned me not to.

"I can't, Daddy."

"Margaret . . . Get. In. The. Car."

Without thinking, I blurted out, "Mama said, 'Don't go'!"

Daddy squinted at me. "What did you say?"

My heart pounded like a racehorse.

"How did she tell you not to go?"

I swallowed, knowing I could never tell him about the Ouija board. "She talks to me sometimes. She doesn't like Miss Muriel."

He pursed his lips in disgust. "Margaret, that's a bunch of horseshit. Now get in the car."

The heavy door groaned in complaint and slammed shut with a similar protest. I rested my head on it, face pressed against the window. The cool glass comforted my formerly defiant and now defeated cheek. I was going to Muriel's house; I wasn't getting out of it. I hoped Mama would understand. I knew Daddy wouldn't.

At Muriel's table, I sulked but kept my manners, sitting slumped-shouldered and blank-faced, not taking part in the conversation. Muriel chirped as she served leg of lamb with mint jelly, mashed potatoes swimming in butter, and snap peas from her backyard, plumped by the hot Louisiana sun. This kind of supper was usually reserved for a special day like Christmas or Easter, but for Muriel it was normal, not fussy or off limits. Passing the peas, I decided she now had two redeeming qualities.

"Did you know armadillos and humans are the only animals that can get leprosy?" I asked Muriel.

Daddy choked on his meat and took a sip of water. He glared at me, but I ignored him.

"I'm not sure what that says about humans," I continued, "but the only armadillos I ever see are the roadkill ones. Have you ever seen them around here?"

Muriel glanced at Daddy, then swiftly steered the conversation away from dead animals. "Jimmy tells me you haven't gone to church in a while."

"No, ma'am."

"Well, you're invited to come to church with your Daddy some Sunday if you'd like."

"Thank you," I said, wishing they would go back to talking to each other and leave me alone.

Muriel tried again. "Do you always go by Margaret?"

I swirled the butter on top of my potatoes. "Yes, ma'am,

but I think Margaret is such a plain name. Mary Queen of Scots, now that's a name. Title, status, where she lived, all of it rolled into one. If I changed my name to Margaret of Thibodaux, everyone would know who I was."

Daddy laughed. I thought it was partly from relief that I hadn't said anything hostile. "People don't use names like that anymore. Now we have first and last names, and you don't need to say where you're from."

"But Daddy, if I meet somebody new, one of the first things they ask me is where I'm from. Why can't I put it in my name, and then everyone will know?"

"You can't, that's all." He softened his tone. "How about if I call you Margaret of Thibodaux? Would that make you happy?"

"Yes, Daddy, it would."

"Do you know what the name Margaret means?" Muriel asked, coming between us.

"No, ma'am." I continued swirling my potatoes with butter until they were almost soup.

"It comes from a Persian word, 'morvared,' which means pearl."

"How do you know that?" Daddy fawned. "We named her for Veone's crazy aunt Margaret, who smoked cigars and wore men's clothes. I didn't know it would have an effect . . ."

Daddy caught my glare and stopped talking.

"Do you know how pearls are made?" Muriel asked.

I turned to her, giving Daddy the cold shoulder. "Pearls come from oysters."

"That's right. The oyster covers an irritating grain of

sand that accidentally made its way into the shell with layer after layer of mother of pearl until it becomes a gem."

The way Muriel spoke, like a kindhearted teacher, allowed a curious warmth of kinship to creep in. But it didn't last. The warning from the Ouija board popped into my mind and I closed down in teenage defiance.

I returned my attention to my plate and sawed the meat as if I was killing it. As I cut it into smaller and smaller bites, I took perverse glee in what I sensed was Daddy and Muriel's worry. Muriel couldn't win me over with one sweet-sounding explanation. I wanted her to have to work hard for me to like her. It made me feel powerful.

Daddy cleared his throat. "There's a festival at the church next week."

I felt the reprieve from their attention as Muriel, her voice bright and bird-like, said that all of us should go.

Daddy agreed, but I would not be attending that function either.

On the drive home, the silence was stiff and unfamiliar.

Before heading upstairs to my room, I kissed Daddy on the cheek—but he didn't smell like Daddy. Instead he smelled like "girlfriend" cologne, not the Old Spice he usually wore.

Hoping to smooth out the dinner awkwardness, I said, "Daddy, did you know Honey calls us 'the Bachelors'?"

"She does? Why?"

"Because you let me keep my room messy and don't make me dress like a girl. It's not really the correct term, though. You're a widower, and I'm a girl, but she couldn't find any other word that described us, so, 'Bachelors.'"

Daddy laughed at most things Honey said and did, but this time he didn't.

"When Miss Muriel moves in after the wedding, you'll have to be neat. Can you do that?"

"Did you know there's no word for a parent who's lost a child?"

Daddy stared at me.

"There also isn't a word for a child who's lost only one parent or a child who has lost a sibling."

Daddy swallowed hard.

"But I'll be sure to keep my room neat for Muriel."

I turned and took the steps to my bedroom two at a time without waiting for a reply.

Chapter 13

Saturday, July 20, 1974

As the sun peeked through the trees, Daddy whistled and rustled around in the kitchen downstairs. He usually slept late on Saturdays, but he was up and busy. As I dressed and went down for breakfast, the smell of bacon and eggs danced up to greet me.

"Morning, Daddy."

"Hi, MOT," he teased with a grin.

He'd already set the table with toast, butter, jam, and orange juice, plus coffee at his place setting. I appreciated him making me breakfast and savored everything he'd made as we talked about the weather and how the frogs were bad this year. Daddy said he'd found a baby snake in the garage and to be careful. Then he said, "Hey, there's something we need to talk about."

The tone of his voice set the hairs on the back of my neck

on end. I had stood to put my plate in the sink but dropped back down, hoping this had nothing to do with Muriel. I was not ready for her so early in the morning.

"May I have a cup of coffee first?" I asked.

He frowned at me and shook his head. Then he took both plates to the sink. When he came back to the table, he pushed in his chair and stood behind it.

"I know you act like you don't like Miss Muriel very much, but I need to know if you really don't like something or if you just think you shouldn't."

A swimming sensation filled my head and tears came. "I don't like her," I said.

Daddy sighed. "We want to include you in this, but you have to be grown up about it."

A voice should sound different talking about death or love, but Daddy's voice sounded the same as it had when he'd told me Mama was dead. It was like hearing the news all over again. He should have loved Mama more.

I raised my face to Daddy's, defiant and blaming, and repeated, "I don't like her."

"Margaret, we're getting married whether you like it or not. We've agreed on a date, but we wanted to ask you to include you too. It's September seventh."

"Two months?" I jumped from my seat. Looking him straight in the eye, I said things a girl should never say to her father, then bolted for the back door.

"Don't you run away from me!" Daddy said.

I sprinted to the bayou, crossed the footbridge to the east, and then headed south to the sugarcane fields. I could hide from the world there, catch my breath. I made it to Laurel Valley Road, but it was already so hot out that I changed my mind about going all the way out to the plantation buildings. The rows of sugarcane surrounded me on both sides of the road, shoulder tall, shushing as the breeze meandered through the stalks. I turned down one of the dirt access roads and hit a muddy patch that hadn't dried yet from yesterday's rain.

Daddy would pull up beside me in the Dart and guilt me into getting in with him. I would make him drive me into town for a vanilla ice cream as a peace offering before we got back to the house and started over from before the fight began.

I slowed my pace and listened for the sound of his car sputtering behind me, but the hum of bugs surrounding me drowned out everything else. The sweet, grassy smell of the cane stalks mixed with the earthy smell of the dirt that nourished them. I pulled air into my lungs, grateful for sensations pushing out thoughts of Daddy and Muriel and Mama.

I rested my hands on my knees and my hair fell in straggly chunks around my face. All I saw was the tops of my Chuck Taylors, covered in mud and disrespected by my attitude.

"Fool," I said aloud to nobody. Talking to myself made me feel like I wasn't crazy when it was exactly the thing that would have made anyone watching think I was.

No Dart. No Daddy.

I was out here sweltering, dressed in rolled-up-to-my-knees jeans and a shirt that would need to soak for two days before anyone would believe it had once been white. I'd made a statement by running away, but Daddy turned his back on me and ignored it.

"Fool!" I raised my voice this time with no ladylike meekness. For ten whole minutes, I stood on the road shouting the word "Fool." My voice bent the cane backwards in fear as I varied the tone, timbre, length of the "oo" and force of the "f," making little bits of spit fly out when I made the "f" low and guttural.

Still no Dart.

The only way I was getting home was Chuck Taylor, and he was not motor-driven. Yelling for a while in the scorching sun had taken the bite out of me, so I turned and shuffled back the way I'd come.

I let the screen door slam behind me as I entered the kitchen. I was going all the way today, so what the hell.

"Hello," I called as if home from school, not back after an argument that had ended with hurtful words, including "hate," "running away," and, worst of all, saying I wished it were Daddy and not Mama who was dead.

I hadn't meant that part. It was the thing I was most sorry for. Daddy once said that everyone hates someone they love sometimes. Even grown-ups wish they could run away, if for only an hour, but no one should ever wish someone was dead.

"In here," Daddy called from the living room. The TV was so soft that I couldn't make out what show was on. It was usually louder, which meant he'd been listening for me. His voice played the game of going back to before the fight; the two words he spoke to me showed no tone of anger.

I walked into the room and sat on the fancy green couch, the one reserved for guests. It was not directly across from his chair, so I had a wide-open path to the kitchen and the stairs should I need to escape.

Daddy turned toward me. "I don't want to reward you for acting like you did, but I thought about it, and I called Miss Muriel to ask her about moving back the wedding to spring. She actually said she was relieved. I guess I was being a little pushy with her too. So, March 22nd. Can you accept March? Can you two get to know each other better before then?"

I didn't want to accept it. I hadn't been able to ask Mama if I should let Daddy get married, but I couldn't delay agreeing to behave and let the engagement continue. I wouldn't say anything about us getting to know each other better, though.

I sat silent for a while, wanting him to squirm with the same discomfort I felt.

He rested his right arm on the chair and cleared his throat a few times, then he rubbed his eyebrow with his middle finger in the spot he'd made bare, a nervous tic left over from the war.

The words wouldn't come that I accepted what was happening. Instead, I got up and kissed him on the cheek, then stuck out my hand to offer him the sign of peace.

"Truce," was all I said.

Daddy accepted both gestures and clasped my hand for a few seconds longer than one would for a strictly social handshake.

"Truce," he replied.

Chapter 14

Wednesday, July 31, 1974

When Daddy got home for supper, I had a feast prepared. He hung his hat by the door and set his lunch pail on the kitchen counter, then took a deep inhale of the distinct smells in the air as he followed me into the formal dining room. Two place settings fit for Thanksgiving graced our spots at the table, accompanied by buttermilk biscuits, flat steak, corn, and mashed potatoes.

"Wow. What's the occasion?" he asked.

"No occasion. I felt like making a feast."

We sat and I bowed my head for grace. After "amen" Daddy said, "Well, you know it's the feast day of St. Ignatius Loyola?"

I stopped with the fork halfway to my mouth. "It is? He keeps showing up. Huh."

Daddy mumbled something as he dug into the meal, but I didn't respond.

After a few silent minutes of buttering biscuits and Daddy shoveling his food at his normal speed-demon pace, I said, "Tell me about the war, Daddy."

He choked on his biscuit. "Where did that come from?"

"When I was grounded, and had all that time to think, I realized the only thing I knew about it was the spot on your brow that you rub. You said it was left over from the war."

Daddy's posture shifted and he stiffened. "What do you want to know?"

Reading his body language, I said, "If you don't want to talk about it, it's fine."

"No, I appreciate the question. I just haven't talked about it before."

I was wondering if it was such a good idea for me to ask when he said, "Well, Robert's dad was in my platoon . . . and we became friends."

I dropped my biscuit. "What? You know Robert's dad? Where is he? Why isn't he here? How did they end up next door to us?"

Daddy ignored my barrage of questions. "We didn't meet until we were in-country. He was a replacement. Bobby Pennington. Robert is named after him." Daddy scooped a mound of mashed potatoes into his mouth. "He was the hardest-working guy I ever met."

"You keep saying 'was.' Is he dead?"

"No."

"Oh man, you're hard to get information out of. Where is he?"

Daddy swallowed and grabbed another biscuit. "It's not for me to say. Robert knows. He can tell you if he wants to."

"Okay, that's fair. But how did they end up next door?"

"I bought the house two weeks after Veone died. I wanted them close, and they needed somewhere safe to live."

"Wait. We own Robert's house?"

"No, *I* own Robert's house. I'm giving it to them when it's paid off."

I didn't understand. Daddy never seemed terribly friendly to Mrs. Pennington or overtly interested in Robert. If the words had not come straight from his mouth, I wouldn't have believed them.

Daddy added, "I thought after all these years of you being friends that his dad would have come up in conversation."

I searched my memory for a time Robert might have tried to tell me something about his family, but I realized, partly and then completely, that I'd never thought to ask him. I'd been so wrapped up in my own life that it hadn't occurred to me other people had stories too.

Dinner didn't feel like a feast anymore, and I was glad when Daddy finished before me and offered to do the dishes.

"Thank you for such a fine dinner," he said.

"You're welcome." I said, displaying uncharacteristic word efficiency. "Daddy?"

"What, Pea?"

"Robert's dad—what did he do for you to be so kind to them?"

Daddy stared into the sink. "He saved my life. Dove into

the water in a swamp when my boot got stuck and we started taking fire. Worked underwater for over a minute. I'd stepped into part of an old ox harness, and it snagged my boot heel in the thick mud and shallow water. I lay down in the water to keep from getting hit, but with my ruck on, I'd never have gotten myself out. Bobby saved me. Selfless. I thought I owed him a little something, and the opportunity presented itself."

"But what happened to him—what was the opportunity?"

Daddy met my eyes. "It's more Robert's place to tell you. It's a bit complicated, and I don't want to step over any lines."

"We don't have any lines," I said. "I'll ask him. He's off grounding, finally."

Daddy dried his hands and leaned against the kitchen counter, studying me.

"Do we have any lines?" he asked.

I studied him back. He looked younger, relaxed, happy.

We didn't have lines. We had walls. Put in place by him. "No, Daddy," I lied.

The following Saturday, Honey was due at the Girls Club. Her mother hadn't abandoned the idea of new friends—which left Robert to me alone, and I was going to make excellent use of the time.

I skipped next door, conscious of keeping things light in case whatever transpired was heavy.

Robert answered the door holding two baseball gloves.

"Bye, Mama! Margaret and I are goin' to play catch!" He didn't wait for an answer before shutting the door and handing me a glove. I held it up to my nose like I always did. Leather gloves and mimeograph sheets—I loved the smell of both.

We headed down to the Talking Tree where there was room to throw. We had enough space in our backyards, but catch with no prying eyes was the better option.

I'd intended to start conversation with, "Hey, my daddy told me at dinner the other night that he knows your dad. How about that?" But instead I blurted out, "So, where's your dad?"

I couldn't control the directness gene, and it expressed itself in severe fashion sometimes.

Robert spun toward me and continued walking sideways. "Where did that come from?"

He sounded defensive.

"Daddy. I asked him to tell me about the war a few nights ago, and he said that's where he met your dad. He said your dad saved his life, but he wouldn't tell me where he is now. Says it's for you to tell me if you want to."

Robert turned forward again and threw the ball into his glove on repeat.

"You don't have to tell me. I'm sorry if it's a sore spot. I never even thought to ask. Daddy says he's alive."

Robert stared into his glove, the motion of his arm his only comment, the sound of the ball hitting the leather his punctuation. Finally, he said, "He's in prison."

My breath rushed out, but luckily no sound came with it.

The thoughts in my head were so jumbled that anything I said would have been gibberish.

"He's in Angola."

Even I knew Angola was an awful place.

"He didn't do anything wrong. Saved someone's life, like he did for Mr. Jimmy."

"Then how is he in prison? What the hell happened?"

My directness seemed to open Robert's reticent gates.

"He was working for this old, angry white man in Iberville Parish. The man was a jerk, and my dad only worked there because he paid well and stayed out of Dad's way. Dad was doing some brickwork on the house and repairing a few of his outbuildings. Anyway, one day, the old man needed to go to the county courthouse, and he asked my dad to drive him. They were going along, and a giant feral hog ran out into the road. Dad swerved to avoid it and ended up in the bayou. The wreck knocked the old man unconscious, and Dad pulled him out of the water to safety. When someone came along a few minutes later, the old man told them my dad tried to kill him . . . that he drove into the bayou on purpose, knocked him on the head with something, and was going to leave him for dead. He said all the money he had in his pocket was gone. They didn't find it on my dad, but it didn't make any difference. The man's wife testified he had two thousand dollars in his pocket the day before that he was going to pay taxes with. I bet he gambled it away and used my dad as a scapegoat."

I let the words settle around us, binding us with a secret, or at least information that wasn't common knowledge.

"Does Honey know?"

He twisted the ball into his glove. "She knows."

"You mean, you told her and not me?"

Robert shrugged. "She asked. Plus her mother is the lawyer working on his appeal."

"Oh," I said.

"Mama and I don't talk about him much. She goes to visit him, but she says I'm too young to go into that environment. We write letters, though. He always says he's going to get out, but it doesn't feel like it will ever happen."

He resumed pummeling the ball into his mitt. "Helping people only brings you trouble."

We continued walking in silence and I didn't ask any more questions. Instead, I said, "It was brave what he did."

Robert shrugged again. "There's a fine line between brave and stupid. I think maybe he crossed it."

What else could I say? Robert's dad was inaccessible, as was Mama. Now the door was open. If Robert wanted to talk, I would listen.

When we got to the Talking Tree, we didn't stop to swing and talk like we usually did. Instead, we threw the ball, and I could tell by the sting in the palm of my hand that Robert wasn't rid of the anger yet. I wasn't very coordinated at some things, but I was good at catching the ball, which probably saved me from getting a black eye. Robert was twenty feet away, but even at that distance, I noticed a tear on his cheek as it caught the summer sun.

I heard a low rumble and both Robert and I looked toward

the street. It was David driving by in his Mustang with his two buddies. I didn't even know their names. Didn't matter. All I saw was David. Robert tipped his head David's way, and David nodded back. They were in the same grade and played baseball together, so it was an acquaintance-type greeting—not friends, not enemies. Robert spent time with his guy friends, but he chose Honey and me just as often. I never asked why.

I was still gawking at David when Robert turned to me. "Don't be lookin' at him that way."

I bit my lip, wondering exactly what face I'd been making. If Robert noticed, had David too?

"I wasn't looking at him 'that way.' I was looking at that handsome mustang."

Robert accepted my lie, probably because I was quick with it.

"He's an okay guy, but he hangs with the wrong crowd." Then he added, "Leave it," as if I was a dog who picked up an unapproved toy.

Not wanting to dig myself a deeper hole, I stuck out my tongue and threw the ball as hard as I could. "I can take care of myself."

The pop into his glove made my point.

After a few more throws, I tossed out a plea. "Would you help me do something if I asked?"

"I thought you could take care of yourself."

I gave him my best scrunched-up face. "Ha Ha." I hurled one back. "I'm serious. You're the only person I can ask."

That got his attention. "What is it?"

"Go with me to Jezebel's house?"

He wound up like a Major League pitcher. "Seems like that's a by-yourself kind of thing. I don't want any trouble gettin' involved with a Voodoo Woman." He let go of the pitch, and the sting hit more than my hand.

Honey wouldn't help me because of her fear of evil, and now Robert wouldn't help me because helping only brought trouble. I was on my own.

Chapter 15

Monday, August 5, 1974

By Monday, I'd figured out a way to get Honey and Robert to go with me to Jezebel's. Sort of.

Jezebel's house was on the corner of Menard and Goode, three streets down from mine, so I suggested a game of spy. We dressed in black to facilitate hiding in the dark, and we carried flashlights, but only for use in an emergency. At fourteen and sixteen, we still played kid games, but now we stayed out past dark. Although our clothes might have hidden us, we giggled and ran into things too often to be anywhere near stealthy.

That night, we'd been running around the neighborhood aimlessly until I casually said, "Let's get closer to Jezebel's house."

Robert was suddenly game. "Let's see if we can peek in her windows."

Honey and I looked at each other, then back at Robert. He had said he didn't want to get involved with Jezebel, and here he was tempting me toward her windows. Before I could say anything, Robert cajoled, "Come on, it'll be easy. The other option is for Margaret to go knock on her door."

"Oh, no," I said. "I'm not doing that. Let's just do the spying thing." I wanted the approach to Jezebel to be a smooth glide, not a hard landing. "If it feels too weird, I'll have to find someone else." Honey's head spun toward me, and I realized I'd inadvertently told her my plans.

She crossed herself and then her arms, trying to keep the evil she imagined at bay.

Robert bolted ahead, stopped, and listened. Then he waved Honey and me forward. Mr. and Mrs. Truman were rocking on their porch. Honey and I both got the giggles and had to look away from each other as we scurried past them.

Jezebel's was the only house on the block with white pickets protecting it. We sneaked to the side, where light filtered through the shaded windows and Jezebel's Confederate jasmine grew in long tendrils. We had to push it aside to get close enough. The perfume it gave off calmed me, but it made Honey sneeze. I shushed her with a finger to my lips as Robert got down on his hands and knees. I climbed on his back to see through the window.

Honey whispered, "Someone's coming!"

A cat moved through the hedge of the house next door. Robert snickered, and I tipped over, falling onto the grass without a sound.

Honey closed her eyes and stiffened. "She knows we're here," she whispered in her best spy voice. "She's gonna jump out of the bushes and scare me to death."

"No, she's not," said Robert. Then he turned to me. "I don't think you're brave enough to spy on Jezebel."

I sat up and crossed my arms at the insult.

Robert continued baiting me. "I dare you to go knock on her door."

I squinted. "We weren't planning to do that. All we wanted to do was *see* her. Prove she exists. I don't want to knock on her door."

"You afraid?"

"No. I'm not afraid of any Vodou woman."

"Okay, then, Wednesday night. You go to her house and knock on her door."

"I can't go there at night. That would be . . . rude. How about Saturday morning?"

"All right, Saturday, it is. Honey and I'll watch from across the way."

"Oh, no. You can't watch. It might make me laugh, and then she'll curse me."

"Fine," Robert said. "But we want proof."

"Proof. What do you want for proof?"

He stood up. "A gris gris bag."

"What the hell is a gris gris bag?"

"It's got herbs and things in it."

"Oh? How do you know that?"

"We live in Louisiana. How do you not know that?"

A screech echoed down the street and we all turned toward it.

"What was that?" I asked, my voice trembling.

"Just an owl," Robert teased. "Don't be such a chicken."

In the shadow of the streetlamp, the way the light hit Robert in profile, I couldn't help but notice how different he was from the pudgy, curly-headed kid I'd met after Mama died. He was even taller—and thinner—than when we'd made the nitroglycerine in June, if that was possible. His voice was deeper too. The way he teased me for being afraid made him seem much older than me, but at least the two of us still towered over Honey.

"So, you'll both help me?"

"Help you with what?" Honey and Robert said in unison, then grinned at each other.

"Jezebel. Talking to Mama."

Robert studied the ground and shook his head. "This is as far as I go."

"Me too," said Honey. "I really don't like talking to spirits and voodoo women and the whole thing. Why do you need our help?"

"What do I say to her? Can I just show up on her doorstep and say, 'Hi, will you help me talk to my dead mother?' I need cheerleaders. I thought that's what friends did for you." I realized as it came out of my mouth that it was the wrong thing to say and quickly backpedaled. "I'm sorry. I'm not friends with you so you'll do something for me."

"It's alright," Honey and Robert echoed again. Then

Robert added, "So all you need is 'Rah rah, go talk to Jezebel'? I could do that, I think."

I raised my brow at Honey.

"Nope. Can't even do that."

I sighed but gave in to a rare moment of generosity. "I understand. Just please don't stop being my friend because I'm doing something you don't like."

"Never even occurred to me," Robert said.

Honey noticed me staring, waiting for an answer from her. "I'm thinking," she said.

For once, I was patient with her because it really did look like she was trying to figure something out.

Finally, she said, "Okay, I don't approve, but I accept that you need to do this. Is that good enough?"

I gave her a quick squeeze. "From you, Honey, it's the best I could hope for."

Chapter 16

Saturday, August 10, 1974

I slowed my pace as I neared my destination, my footfalls sloshing on the wet sidewalk as I stepped in every puddle on the way. I would go see Mama even if prison was her residence. I'd go see her in heaven too if I could figure out how without dying first.

The walk to Jezebel's door was lined with short white pickets, which symbolized welcoming and normalcy. Then my eye caught a chicken skeleton perched on the roof of the front porch. I'd never noticed it before, and I wished I hadn't noticed it now.

I thought of Robert teasing me for "chickening out" and had to laugh. Still, I paused before scaling the steps.

I knocked lightly on Jezebel's door. I heard footsteps, then hesitation. When she opened the door, her mouth was puckered in displeasure. She narrowed her eyes as she looked me up and down.

"*Comment ça va?*" she said in French.

"*Ça va bien, et vous?*" I replied, proud that I'd remembered the formal phrase I was supposed to use when meeting someone older than me for the first time. "I'm Margaret. I live a few blocks from you." I turned and pointed to my house.

"I know who you are, child. Does your fa'der know you come to see me?"

"No. He lets me go where I want as long as I come home for supper when he whistles."

She studied me for a few more seconds then nodded. "'Dat seems fair. Come in."

The house smelled of chicken like Robert said it would. Another scent was mixed with it, something pungent and unfamiliar, like garlic, but not quite. Beads hung above a doorway into another room but she didn't lead me through them. Instead, she motioned for me to sit on the gold-and-brown flowered couch.

"No one comes to my house anymore," she said. "Why you here?"

The shades were drawn so none of the morning light filtered in; the room was dark except for several lamps with gold silk shades that cast an amber light. My eyes hurt struggling to focus after being in the sunlight.

"I thought I should visit you since we've been neighbors for so long." I moved a few pillows aside and scooted near the arm of the couch for protection.

Jezebel sat across from me in a large wooden rocking chair. "Your mama tell you to come here?"

"My mama's dead."

Jezebel's face softened. "I know. 'Dat's why I asked you. Did she say come?"

My heart leapt then started pounding. *She knew.*

This was the first time I'd met anyone like me, someone who believed that existence extended beyond the physical.

"No. Yes. I mean, no. She didn't say for me to come here."

I fiddled with my hands. I was at Jezebel's under false pretenses. Even though I wanted her help, I had come on a dare. I couldn't start out with deception.

I stood. "I need to be going. I'm sorry to have bothered you."

Jezebel rocked calmly. With my eyes adjusted, I noticed she wore a single-strand pearl necklace like the one Mama had on in some of her pictures. It was out of place with the brightly colored loose dress she wore over her wispy thin body.

"No bo'der. What you want to know about your mama?"

I shifted my weight and swallowed. "Lots of things. But it's not so much that I want to know something. I want to be able to talk to her. I was hoping you could teach me how."

"You sure 'dat's what you want to learn?"

A grain of fear worked its way up my arms. I hadn't considered that she might refuse. Jezebel was my last resort.

"My friends won't help me. No one will . . . except you."

She considered her hands, splayed out on the arms of the rocker. The clock ticked.

"Will you help me? Learn to talk to Mama, I mean?"

Jezebel rose with the grace of a black leopard moving through the forest and came to me. She was an inch or two taller than me, so it was easier now to look her in the eyes. Hazel. She reached out and touched my arms at my sides, patting them gently.

"You 'tink talking to her helps you?"

I nodded. "Yes."

"And what do I get for helping you?"

I hadn't thought about this being a transactional event, but it made sense that it should be. "I can pay you," I offered.

"I don't need money."

"What do you need?"

Jezebel paused for a moment. "Your friends dare you to come?"

I couldn't have been more astonished if I'd seen an actual ghost standing in front of me.

Suddenly, a big, rolling laugh burst from Jezebel.

"I couldn't keep it in!" she said. "Robert asked me to play like I was mad, but I can't do it."

A hot flush crept up my neck and into my face. Robert had set me up. I stared at my Chuck Taylors, wishing the floor would swallow me up.

Jezebel read my stance and softened her laugh. Then she lifted my face up to hers.

"I've known Robert since he was a boy. He never told you he knows me?"

I shook my head. Fear and embarrassment crowded together in my mind. Being face to face with the Vodou woman gave me a dry mouth and shaking hands.

"Let's get him back," Jezebel said.

I spun around to see her cross to a side table and open a narrow drawer, then she strode back over to me. I stood rooted in her living room, afraid to step anywhere for fear of some other unknown. "Take 'dis and tell him I made it of him. Tell him I didn't know who you were and made 'dis voodoo doll from your description." She winked and leaned closer. "You know we don't actually make voodoo dolls, right? 'Dat's 'de movies."

Her conspiratorial eyes told me I could play along and there was nothing to fear.

I took the doll but hesitated. "How did you know my mama speaks to me sometimes?"

"You know 'tings. I know 'tings. It just comes."

"How do you make it come? Does Vodou do that for you?"

She beamed, perhaps proud I used the correct word. "Yes and no. It's different from what people 'tink. Some of us hear or see 'tings most o'ders don't. You can use it or not, learn more or not. It's a skill."

It had never occurred to me that what I had was a skill. A new curiosity piqued, but my Southern clock of the proper visit length had sounded an alarm in my head, and it was time to leave.

"I'd like to come again, Miss Jezebel, if that's okay."

"Whenever you want, Miss Margaret. *Au revoir.*"

I skipped all the way home with the fake doll in my hand and plans in my head to vex Robert for at least ten minutes. I had to be careful about Honey, though. If she got the wrong idea, she'd pray incessantly for my soul.

Margaret of Thibodaux

In the early evening, I walked to the Talking Tree. Filtered light illuminated the water drifting by at its lazy pace. The bayou gave me the sensation that it listened to my troubles and carried them away.

I was standing at the water's edge, throwing small pebbles into the bayou and enjoying the "plunk" of stone hitting water, when Robert and Honey ran up to me, breathless.

"So, what happened? Was she nice? Was she scary?" Honey smoothed her disheveled hair back into her barrettes. "Well?" she urged.

"She was nice."

"That's it?" Honey huffed. "That's the big report?"

"You sure are interested in someone you aren't interested in," I teased.

"I asked her for a gris gris bag, but she gave me this." I thrust the doll toward Robert. He pulled back his hands and stepped backwards so fast he almost fell. I laughed and gave myself away. Not even ten minutes' worth.

"She told you, didn't she?" Robert shook his head. "Man, I knew she wouldn't be able to keep a straight face. You either."

Honey's mouth hung open. I weighed the fallout of keeping her in the dark. With a glance at Robert, I caught his agreement to let her in on the deception.

"Honey, Jezebel's known Robert all his life. He played a trick on us, tried to scare us with a 'Voodoo' woman. She's really very nice. You'd like her."

Honey stamped her foot like a child. "Not funny. I was all

worried about you getting put under a spell by her, and it turns out to be a big joke."

Robert smiled and put his arm around Honey. "Come on. It was a joke on the both of us. No harm done."

"Well," Honey pouted, "I guess it's all right. But I don't like being scared. Promise you won't scare us anymore, Robert."

"Can't do that," he said with a grin. "So, is she going to help you, Margaret? Are Honey and I off the hook?"

I realized Jezebel had invited me back, but she hadn't given me an answer.

"How's she going to help you?" Honey prodded. "Do you have to learn voodoo?"

"It's not voodoo; it's Vodou. But she said it's not Vodou that lets you talk to spirits. It's a skill."

"Oh."

"I'm going back tomorrow."

It wasn't a lie. I needed it to be true that Jezebel would help.

Chapter 17

Sunday, August 11, 1974

The next morning, I knocked on the door of the tidy yellow house. It was Sunday, so Honey couldn't intervene to save my soul.

Jezebel invited me in. Although the shades were still closed, the living room seemed brighter.

"Why do you have a chicken skeleton on your roof?" I asked.

"It's funny. And it keeps 'de riffraff away."

I realized I might be riffraff, whatever that was.

Jezebel motioned me into her living room.

"Where are you from?" I asked, taking a seat on the gold-flowered couch.

"Haiti. Moved to Louisiana twenty years ago."

"What's it like? Haiti?"

"It's beautiful and terrible. 'De beautiful is 'de wild, 'de plants, 'de animals, 'de ocean. 'De terrible is 'de poverty. Hopeless, mean people sometimes. When I was a child, I worked cutting cane in 'de fall and helped my mother wit' my twelve brothers and sisters 'de rest of 'de time. It's nice to live alone."

I loved listening to her talk. Her words were recognizable but different from my own, the structure and accent making the language unique, melodic, and mesmerizing. The French influence was obvious when she sprinkled in words that had a French sound, or used French words instead of English. I followed most of it. Cajun and Creole folks were common in Thibodaux, and I'd listened to patois for as long as I could remember. There was a lilt to their speech, and maybe to mine too. Most of the time, I didn't even notice when folks dropped their th's and substituted d's or t's, or when the lady in the grocery store asked me to give her regards to Zh'immy.

"Miss Jezebel, why did you move here?"

"I had no choice in 'de matter."

I laughed. "You don't seem like you do anything against your will."

"I had an old Tantine lived here and needed some looking after, and I needed to get away from home. So, Manman sent me. Here I am, and Tantine is long gone."

"What did you need to get away from at home?"

She drew her head back. "'Dat's a story for ano'der day," which likely meant never.

I got the hint and changed topics. "What's Vodou?"

"It's a religion. We worship one God, but we are active; we serve. I was around it a lot as a child. I don't do much now except for healing."

"How come in the movies, Vodou is a bad thing?"

"Because 'dey don't understand it. You make some'ting you don't understand be bad. You Cat'olic?"

"Yeah, I think so. I mean, I believe in God and everything. I try to be a good Catholic, being nice and doing unto others. I give myself a B, some days an A-minus."

Jezebel laughed. "Sounds good. You like some sweet tea?"

"Yes, please."

She disappeared through the beaded doorway, then swished back through a few minutes later with two glasses and handed me one. "It's a nice day. Let's sit outside."

I followed her to the back porch and sat next to her on the swing. Jezebel's billowing dress swept the wood as we moved back and forth.

"Many who practice Vodou are also Cat'olic," she said.

I sipped the tea and searched my memory for any stray mention of Jezebel at Mass, but found none. Jezebel must have read my mind because she patted my leg and said, "I go to a church in Belle Rose on Saturday evenings. Have for years."

That explained why she was never at Mass at St. Joseph's. "How can you be Catholic and a Vodou . . . ite?"

"It's been 'dat way for a real long time."

"So, what's the difference?"

"Too many to name, baby."

I loved it when older women called me baby. It was a comfort I couldn't describe. I was comfortable here too. It made no sense that this lady with a different culture and customs seemed familiar, but I felt it deep inside. And if Jezebel had my same gift, she could teach me how to deal with it, Catholic or no, Vodou or no.

I swiveled toward her. "How do I talk to Mama?"

Jezebel kept swinging and sipping her tea. I thought she hadn't heard me.

"Jezebel, how do I—"

"I heard you," she interrupted, then fell silent again.

I fidgeted with the buttons on my shirt.

She shifted to face me. "It's a big question. No magic pill or action lets you control it. You have to learn, and it takes a long time."

I swallowed hard at the bad news. "You see, I don't have a lot of time. I have questions for her now."

Jezebel patted my hand and turned back to the yard stretching before us. The sweet smell of grass rose as the sun warmed the ground. We swung in silence while I gathered more questions.

"Can you talk to her for me?" I asked.

"No."

Silence again.

"Do you talk to any spirits—on purpose, I mean?"

Jezebel took a deep breath, as if she was going underwater for an unknown length of time.

"I can call on 'de lwa, 'de spirits, much like 'de saints, for guidance, but I don't communicate wit' 'dem like some can, like you can."

"But I can't really. Not on purpose. How do I talk to Mama on purpose? Ask her questions?"

Jezebel took a sip of her tea. "You know what 'meditation' is?"

"I read about it in a book recently."

"Good. First 'ting you learn 'den. Set up a quiet, comfortable place in your room. Find some'ting to help you focus—flame of a candle, tick of a clock, some'ting like 'dat. 'Den you sit and focus and relax. Next, imagine yourself sitting on 'de beach and let people walk by. Pay attention to 'dem and write down what you see."

I nodded and breathed in, tasting the fresh-cut grass. Sitting with Jezebel like this was lovely.

"Tell me about the Ouija board."

Jezebel jerked her head toward me, dissipating my comfort in an instant.

"Don't ever do 'dat," she said, her tone serious.

I bit my lip. "It's too late. We did it last month." I smiled to brighten the now dense atmosphere.

"*Mon Dieu*," Jezebel whispered, crossing herself like Honey did when certain words came out of my mouth. "Promise me to never touch 'dat 'ting again. Promise."

"Okay, sheesh, I won't do it. It didn't let me talk to Mama anyway."

"Because it's 'de base spirits, 'de lowest ones come 'tru 'dere." Jezebel made chuffing noises and continued grumbling to herself. "I wish you come to me before you do 'dat. Don't ever do 'dat."

"I didn't know you then."

"No matter. Don't ever do it again."

Forgetting my manners, I said, "I heard you the first three times."

"And I'm gonna say it again." She raised her voice at me for the first time. I didn't think it would be the last. "Don't ever do 'dat evil 'ting again, or I won't help you. It's not a game."

Her message came through loud and clear, but I still had questions.

"How is it evil?"

Jezebel sat back. "'De spirit world is complicated."

I waited for more.

"Every'ting in existence vibrates. 'De rock, it vibrates slow. 'De water, it vibrates a little faster. 'De air, it vibrates fastest." Jezebel shook her hands to illustrate each state of matter: close together and barely moving for rock, wider apart and faster for water, and waving around wildly for air.

I laughed at her pantomime, but she quieted me with a stare.

"'De human body made up of solid and water. 'De spirit made up like air. Communication is difficult if 'de vibrations are so different."

"But isn't water kind of in the middle? We're almost seventy percent water. My friend, Honey, said so."

Jezebel smiled, and her face lit up. "'Dat's right. 'Dat's 'de next 'ting I was gonna say. Our bodies are built to communicate if we want. It's a lost art. If we concentrate and practice, we can use middle vibrations to reach 'de spirits. But you have to believe you can do it. 'Dat's why meditation is helpful. You must practice. Now, here's your homework. Next week, you bring me notes about what meditation show you, even if it don't seem like much. Okay?"

I took the assignment like I took my math homework, befuddled as to the why and how, but determined to find the answer.

Chapter 18

Monday, August 12, 1974

Piggly Wiggly had an excellent assortment of candles, but I decided to buy a plain white one. A devotional candle for church seemed perfect to help me focus and relax. I wondered as I paid the cashier if anyone else misused a candle the way I intended to.

When I got home, I made a little space on the floor between my bed and the window and threw down some pillows, then I placed the candle on the windowsill and lit it. I sat on the pillows and leaned against the bed. The wood beams above my head were rough and dusty. I closed my eyes and waited for blank to appear, but all I saw were black and red spots on the inside of my eyelids, same as when I closed my eyes for sleep. I tried staring at the candle flame, but it made my eyes cross and gave me a headache, so I imagined a beach like Jezebel said.

The beach built itself up, layer by layer: first the sand,

then the water, then the blue sky. I heard seagulls squawk and smelled the salty water. It was hard to hold the picture for any longer than a few seconds, and I had to start all over if I lost it.

My thoughts wandered to an image of Honey scowling at me. I shook my head like shaking an Etch-A-Sketch to make the picture go away.

It was as quiet as a graveyard in my room. A buzz filled my ears, and I wondered if it had always been there but I'd never noticed it because of the other noises that usually made up my world. I didn't like the space of quiet; it made me uneasy and restless, not relaxed and open, as Jezebel described.

Jezebel said to practice the beach scene and a blank mind so things I didn't know about could seep in, but blank wasn't working for me. I closed my eyes again and dragged my imagination back to the beach, holding it long enough for a few distant people to appear near the water. The sun was high in the sky, and its brightness hurt my eyes. The warm sunlight fell on my face, and I smiled, a drowsy, lid-heavy smile that accepted the light for the gift it was. The water was dark blue at the horizon, then faded and changed to a murky green near the shore. A small band of white drew a line between water and earth where the waves broke on the sand. Now and then, people walked into and then out of my field of vision, small and distant, far from where I sat. The dogs were different. They ran right up and put their wet noses all over my leg as they tried to guess from my scent where I was from and to whom I belonged.

It must have been a California beach, though I had never been there. The sun was setting in the ocean, and that didn't happen near home. The Gulf was the ocean to Louisiana, but the beaches faced south, so I was not there. All Jezebel had said to me was, "Close your eyes and imagine sitting on 'de beach." It was strange that what came to my mind was a vision of a west-facing beach I'd never been to.

The wind blew, and the dune grass bent in waves of supplication to the unseen force. It was like looking out the window at a storm. I became sleepy to the point I felt like I could fall asleep and never wake up. But it wasn't a depressed sleepy or a wanting to escape; I was just relaxed in a way I wasn't used to. As surely as the priest's homily got me drowsy Sunday morning, my head nodded in fits of sleep and wake.

Jezebel had said to concentrate and relax at the same time. I thought about the time I'd gone water skiing with friends one summer near their lake cabin and they'd all shouted pointers from the boat: "Set your skis straight." "Hold the rope close to your chest." "Knees up." I concentrated on one thing at a time, hopelessly uncoordinated in getting my body parts to each do their independently assigned task. It took forever to put all the pieces together and get up out of the water.

I had always had to learn things by doing them over and over again, folding each part and task into the batter of a skill so as to not break up the individual ingredients, yet make something of use for later. That was the arduous task, control over my body and mind. I had grown so fast; I didn't have control of anything. Long legs, knobby knees, and "hands the size of Texas," as Daddy said. My feet were pretty, though.

"Concentrate!" I said aloud as my thoughts wandered to inconsequential things.

When I opened my eyes, I realized I'd drifted off. The candle was still lit but had burned down a third. The flash of fear that I'd been sleeping with a lit candle made my heart jump.

I stared at the flame for a minute before closing my eyes and discovered it left a ghosted image on my lids. This time, using that as a focus for my concentration, I built up the beach scene. To my amazement, I watched people go by me with ease. From my left, a lithe and graceful woman walked along the waterline, stopping to pick up shells or drag her toe through the sand. She wore a fluttery sundress and wide-brimmed hat. I judged her as beautiful, even from far away, and liked her presence, calm and content.

It was like dreaming, in a way. I did not direct the woman; I just let her actions unfold and waited for something important to happen. When she wandered closer, I realized with a start that it was Muriel.

"Who said you could come into my meditation?" I asked out loud.

The sleepy, dreamy atmosphere was gone. The woman who'd meandered through my meditation contradicted my assessment. Muriel was scheming. Meditation showed her differently.

Chapter 19

Saturday, August 17, 1974

Over the last few days, when I tried to meditate and Muriel kept showing up, I decided I would just ignore her, both in meditation and real life. I'd have to practice it, though. Ignoring someone wasn't in my nature, but a studied indifference might make Daddy realize this was still moving way too fast.

It was Daddy's birthday. Every year I made sure his card was sitting on the table when he came down for his breakfast, then for dinner I made him a T-bone steak and took him out for ice cream afterward at Dairy Queen.

Muriel decided this year would be different.

After Daddy got home from work, I only got to see him for a few minutes, enough time to give him the mustard-colored cable sweater I'd bought at JCPenney. He kissed me on the head and said, "Thank you, Pea," then ran upstairs to change.

Margaret of Thibodaux

Muriel arrived at 6:00 p.m., wearing a blue sheath dress with see-through sleeves and her hair up in a French roll. I greeted her at the door and held out my hand, giving the fish handshake Daddy detested.

"Come in, Miss Muriel. Daddy's not ready yet, but you can sit in the living room."

Muriel smiled and made a move like she was going to hug me, but I reached behind her for the door and closed it instead.

"I'm excited to get to know you better," Muriel said.

I moved my hands to my hips and stood my ground. "I'm excited too," I said with flat affect that exuded no excitement whatsoever.

Daddy must have included the "get to know you better" ingredient when he and Muriel talked after I'd run away. She apparently agreed. I didn't.

Pleasantries exchanged, I waved her toward the living room while I walked into the kitchen, where I banged pots and dishes as I put them away from the drying rack.

Instead of behaving and sitting in the living room as instructed, Muriel followed me into the kitchen. "Can I help?"

"No."

"Jimmy says you're quite the help around the house."

I poured oil into a pot on the stove. "I kind of have to be."

"Well, I can help when . . . after . . . soon."

I scattered popcorn into the bottom of the pot. The noise made it impossible to hear what Muriel said next.

"Sorry?" I said, though I wasn't.

"I said I hope you have a good evening."

"Oh, thank you. You too." Pop. Pop. Pop, pop, pop.

Daddy swept into the kitchen and kissed Muriel hard on the lips. "What are my two best girls talking about?" he said over the bursting of the kernels.

To me, he sounded like he thought Muriel and I were friends already. *Not so fast, buster.* "Nothing," I said, keeping strict attention on the stovetop. I hated burned popcorn.

"I was telling Margaret how much I can help her, and you too." Muriel sounded nervous, trying to fit her words between the flurries of pops.

I was grateful their sweet nothings were drowned out as I melted the butter. Then, in perfect timing, I lifted the lid of the pot and dumped the fluffy, steaming heap into a giant metal bowl. I poured butter all over it followed by a few pinches of salt, then I shook the whole thing like it was a science experiment.

When I swung around with the bowl, Muriel was standing closer than I realized. Even with her black high heels, she only came up to my forehead, giving me the advantage in the size department. To avert a massive spill, I swerved around her and marched into the living room, enjoying the tension. They called their goodbyes from the front door as I stuffed a handful of popcorn into my mouth.

After they left, I switched the channels on the TV, but no story matched my mood. I would get in trouble if I waited up for Daddy, but I decided that telling him I'd lost track of time was only a little fudge of the truth. I had questions that couldn't wait. Popcorn, butter, and salt soothed me temporarily.

At ten fifteen, Daddy turned the key in the lock. I was sitting in his dark brown leather recliner with the TV still on, pretending I'd dozed off. The surprise on his face was enjoyable. I tried to discern if it was from my being up—I never did that—or from my sitting in his chair, which he didn't know I did all the time. *Surprise is better than anger.*

"What are you doing up . . . in my chair?" he asked, capturing both transgressions at once as he hung his hat on the rack.

I moved to the green couch across from Daddy's chair. "I have questions," I said.

He fell into his recliner, tired and ready for bed, not for the barrage I was known to hurl. Still, he said, "Shoot."

His easy agreement set me to pause, and I backed off my initial desire to pummel him. "Why are you marrying Miss Muriel?"

Daddy smiled at her name and relaxed. "Because she said yes."

That was it. No expansion on the idea, no explanation.

"But what about me?"

"What about you?"

"Where do I fit in?"

"Same place you've always been, Margaret."

The conversation was unsatisfactory. I didn't like this unfamiliar distance from my father one bit—the one that started when Muriel entered our lives.

"What about Mama?"

"Mama is dead."

It sounded so cold, a stone added to the many already firmly set in the wall between us.

Daddy turned to switch off the table lamp, and I noticed a glint on his wrist.

"What's that?"

Again, his face lit up, and he stretched his arm out to show me. "New watch. Birthday gift from Miss Muriel."

It looked expensive and far more dear than the sweater I'd given him, hanging forlorn on the back of his chair.

I had to stand up for Mama since she wasn't able to stand up for herself. This was not the natural course of things. Nothing about Muriel was natural, and nothing about her wheedling her way into our family could be construed as respectful of Mama. Muriel schemed, and I was the one to warn Daddy of the danger.

Daddy must have read my mind. "I think we need new rules in the house."

"I do too."

"You are to be respectful to Miss Muriel at all times."

"Wait, what? I am respectful. I shook her hand and everything. What did she tell you?"

"Never mind what Miss Muriel said. I saw how you acted toward her, and it wasn't very welcoming."

"Don't you think I have a right to be suspicious of a lady who waltzes in here and tries to act like we're old friends?" I said it with a little too much of an edge to be respectful to my father, and I braced for his shift in demeanor. But the only change was a curl at the corner of his lip.

"She comes over for our dates instead of letting me pick her up so she can see you too."

I looked away and chewed the inside of my cheek.

"I don't expect much from you, Margaret. Chores, be nice, read, write, and speak proper English. You have an easy life. She's trying so hard to get to know you, and you're not trying at all."

When I didn't respond to his statement, he said, "Well?"

"Well, what?"

"I explained that she comes here to see you too. You don't need to be suspicious if you know why she does something. She's not waltzing, and she's not acting like your old friend. She's acting like a new one."

"Oh, you didn't say that part exactly." I glanced at the floor then back up to Daddy. "What if I don't want her to be my friend?"

"I suppose that's your choice, but you're missing out."

"I think I'll have to risk it for the time being."

Daddy glared at me, but I was getting good at showing my indifference and left him fuming in his chair.

Chapter 20

Monday, August 19, 1974

I'd forgotten to dust on the weekend, so to avoid an argument, I got up early to do more than I usually did—and to make sure Daddy saw me doing it.

When I got to the dining room, a pretty pink rock sat on the sideboard. It was clear in places and angular, but the opposite side was smooth, round, and cloudy pink. I'd never seen anything like it.

Daddy was still reading his paper at the breakfast table.

"What's this?" I asked, the rock lying in my outstretched palm.

"Miss Muriel put it there. She said it's a quartz of some kind. Rose quartz? Rice quartz? I don't remember."

"Why did she give you a rock?"

Daddy laid his paper on the table. "I didn't ask her. She can't move in with us until after the wedding, so maybe she's eager to start bringing some things she loves to her future home."

I was tempted to throw it in the trash when Daddy left for work, but that would be hard to explain, the disappearance of a rock. So, I put it back where I'd found it.

I'd waited and meditated for eight whole days without bothering Jezebel. As soon as I finished my chores, I left the house for my third visit, with more questions than answers.

After exchanging greetings in French, Jezebel ushered me through the pleasant clacking of doorway beads into the kitchen and told me to sit at the small, square table. She took a kettle off the stove and poured hot water into two cups with tea bags draped inside. As she stirred in sugar, two cubes each, I asked, "What's the point of meditation?"

"Quieting your mind," she said, sitting across from me.

"How quiet does it need to be?"

"Quiet enough so you can hear ants crawling on 'de floor . . . or 'de whisper of a spirit who doesn't have much energy to come 'tru 'de veil to communicate."

"Okay, and what does that mean?"

Jezebel steeped and stirred. "When you are spirit, you have energy, you made of energy, but you don't have a body. No physicalness. It takes energy to make a human notice you. Some spirits have more energy 'dan o'ders or more practice at getting your attention."

"So, how come it happens sometimes, but I can't make it happen?"

"We don't always know. Could be 'dey busy and can't come. Could be 'dey don't want to talk to you right 'den. Could be you getting in your own way. 'Dat's how meditation helps. Gets your brain to stop directing 'tings. 'Den you might be able to pick up energy from a spirit."

I moved my tea bag slowly up and down, watching the water become more amber. "Mama sits at my feet, and she sings to me. It must take loads of energy."

"'Dat's right. You remember I told you about 'de water analogy last Sunday?"

I didn't remember any "water analogy." I shook my head.

Jezebel got up and disappeared down the dark hallway. After making noise in another room, she came back with a small paperback book in her hand.

"I like 'dis explanation. Found it in 'dis book." She flipped the pages, her eyebrows touching in concentration. "Ah, here it is."

"All of existence vibrates. Even granite vibrates. Atoms are in constant motion (simplified as vibration), and 'de states of matter are defined by 'dere vibrational level. In general, solids vibrate slowly, liquids vibrate more quickly, and gases vibrate 'de fastest. Elements can exist as solid, liquid, or gas and so can compounds. Water is 'de most recognizable compound and has an important connection as well to 'de human body—so it makes 'de best analogy."

Jezebel looked up to confirm I was paying attention.

"Ice is H20 in a lattice structure, and 'de atoms are vibrating at such low energy 'dey 'buzz' instead of moving perceivable distances like water or steam. Water is H20 in a vibrational state 'dat allows movement, but 'de atoms are still cohesive and close toge'der.

Steam is H2O, but 'de vibrational level is so high 'de atoms dissipate until 'dey are not perceivable. Spirit communication and water states are not exactly 'de same, nor is 'dis meant to be a scientific explanation for how spirit communication happens. Consciousness does not require physicality.

But—when humans die—'de vessel ('de body) is dealt wit' as solid matter. We bury it, cremate it, and it decays. 'De Soul acts like water vapor. We may not be able to see it, but it's 'dere. When I ask spirit to communicate, I'm asking 'dem to use energy to 'condense' enough so I can perceive 'dem in some way—like water vapor condensing enough to be perceived as fog.

For humans, our emotions are a barometer of sorts for our vibrational level. Sadness, grief, and anger are solid level, low vibration, and joy, happiness, and laughter are gas level, high vibration. When you hear it is desirable to raise your vibration—you do 'dis wit' gratitude, happiness, meditation, and laughter. Simple."

Jezebel looked up at me and smiled, then continued reading.

"In order to incarnate, our Souls slow 'dere vibrations to match solid bodies. But humans are not entirely solid. We are sixty percent water.

Water is analogous to 'de communication zone. If we raise our vibration, and spirit lowers 'deres, we meet in 'de middle. Physical water holds 'dis higher vibration because it matches its own physical state.

If we look at how 'de human body, 'de vessel for 'de Soul, is structured, since we are partly water, and we are built to communicate wit' spirit. Our physical bodies are a communication tool. We have to be able to manage a high enough vibration to meet spirit near 'de boundary. 'Dis is also why 'dose in grief, anger, sadness—'dose who need spiritual comfort—often cannot reach 'dat level; 'de difference in vibrational state is too great. 'Dey are at a low, solid vibration level, and spirit is vapor. Quite a chasm to cross.

So, communication wit' spirit is possible. It is part of 'de Divine design."

Jezebel closed the book.

I was stunned. "So we have built-in ability to communicate with spirit? Our bodies are set up that way?"

"Sounds like. Does it make sense to you?"

"I guess so. That's a little over my head, to tell the truth. Do you agree with all that?"

"I don't know much about science, but my experience tells me yes. It's very much like 'dis," she said, patting the cover.

I was still processing this when Jezebel said, "'Dat's enough for today, Miss Margaret." She waved her hand toward the living room and we took our teacups to the more comfortable furniture.

The tea was calming as I scanned the room. It didn't look like a Vodou Woman's house, although I'd never been in one before. It looked—normal. Plates with scenes of buildings or horses stood sentinel on a rail high up on the wall, almost to the ceiling. A picture of Jezebel in her younger days, sitting in a rocking chair on a porch I did not recognize, rested between books and a vase of flowers on a shelf.

"Where was this taken?" I asked, pointing to the picture.

"*Mon Dieu*, 'dat's me at 'de house I grew up in. Just outside Port Au Prince."

"What about there?" I pointed to another picture of Jezebel, this one with a young woman to her left and a handsome young man on her right.

"Paris, 1935. My sister and my husband."

"You never told me about your husband," I said before thinking it through.

"Yes, well, I'm not married now."

"Did he die?"

Jezebel walked over to the picture and laid it face down

on the table. "No, he's alive. He drinks and cannot control his temper. So I left him, twenty years ago." Her posture suddenly reflected an old woman, as if dredging up memories of past hurts weighed her down. I'd insisted on knowing something that wasn't my business, and I wished I could take the questions back.

Within seconds, though, Jezebel sprang back to the lithe and strong woman she was now.

I wished I could do the same—and as swiftly.

Chapter 21

Sunday, August 25, 1974

I practiced meditation for days, sometimes discovering something and sometimes waking up after a nap. I still used the candle to focus, but I did it lying down because it was more comfortable and I didn't have to concentrate on sitting up straight. I didn't know if what happened in meditation was absolute truth, near truth like dreams, or just weird, so I went to Jezebel's that afternoon for more answers.

Like always, she welcomed me in as if she expected me. I took my place on the couch and she settled into her rocker.

"What if I don't believe what happens during meditation?" I asked. "Do spirits fall down dead like Tinker Bell? Wait, they're already dead. Do they 'poof!' just disappear?"

Rocking lightly, she said, "'Tings 'dat are true are true whe'der you believe 'dem or not. God exists and doesn't need you to believe he exists. What you call His energy and how much you believe in Him does not affect Him; it affects you."

"Things that are true are true whether you believe them

or not," I repeated, digesting the words and the concept.

"Your perception is ano'der 'ting." She leaned toward me. "If you and I stand face to face and I say 'dis oak tree is on my right, would you argue wit' me because, clearly, 'de oak tree is on your left? No, because we understand how 'de world works and 'dat my perception is influencing my description of 'de tree. We don't process it consciously because it is accepted concept. However, very few of us, me included, understand how 'de Universe, how Existence works, specifically 'de spirit realm. So much of our communication about it is from our perception of it. It's 'de only way we can communicate some'ting 'dat is beyond our human senses. So, you have to let go of trying to be right about any'ting. Just be."

I fiddled with my hands in my lap. Some of the explanation was flying far above me, beyond my understanding.

"Let me ask you a question. You know how to find where you are if you lost in the wilds?" She didn't wait for me to answer. "No, you probably never even been to New Orleans."

"I have too."

She waved her hand. "No matter. You know how to save yourself if you get lost?" Again, she answered for me. "Triangulation."

"Triangulation. What's that?"

"Triangulation is using 'tree different, immovable points to orient yourself."

"Okay, duly noted for the next time I go camping. But what does that have to do with talking to Mama?"

"'Tink, Margaret. Engage your brain."

I sat back and folded my arms.

Jezebel sighed and stood up. "Come on," she said.

I followed her to the back porch, where we sat on the swing in silence. I watched six minutes tick by on my watch, not thinking at all about what triangulation could mean to me.

Finally, Jezebel said, "You ever have dreams?"

"Yes."

"Can you prove it?"

"They can do brainwave tracings to show you dream." Another data point courtesy of Honey Sinclair.

"Ah, 'dey can show '*dat* you dream, not *what* you dream."

"Same thing, isn't it?"

"Not at all. 'Dey can do brainwaves. You tell 'dem a dream about getting chased by a bear. Can you prove 'dat's what your dream was?"

"No, I guess not."

"So, why people accept what others tell 'dem about dreams? Because we all have 'dem and we know what 'dere like. But spirit, not everyone feels 'dem or sees 'dem. People 'tink it's not true. But you know it's true 'cause it happens to you. 'Dat's where you stand. Now . . . you find 'tree points outside of you 'dat don't change."

I unfolded my arms and sat forward, resting my chin in my hand.

When I didn't come up with a point right away, Jezebel offered, "First triangulation point, your Mama is dead. 'Dat's a fact ain't changing."

I hadn't thought of Mama's death as a point external to me. I'd always imagined it was part of me, but in reality, it wasn't. It was odd but helpful to put her death outside of me for once.

"'Tink about it. Communicating what we perceive to someone else is limited by language and 'de o'der person's understanding. You can tell someone all you want you feel your Mama, but if 'dey never had 'dat experience, ei'der 'dey won't believe you, or 'dey won't understand. A special person believes you and understands. Triangulation point number two."

"Honey believes me, but Daddy doesn't."

"Perfect. 'Dat's actually two different points, on opposite ends. Toge'der wit' your Mama being dead, 'dat makes all 'tree points outside you to bump up against."

"But . . . if all three of those things already exist . . . why am I lost?"

"Because you don't know you *aren't*."

I turned to face her. "Huh?"

"Someone who believes you, who doesn't have to, is a strong and wonderful 'ting. And someone who *doesn't* believe you adds pause to your 'toughts and actions."

"But why is someone else's opinion important for knowing where *I* am?"

Jezebel tipped her head. "Why you 'tink?"

I thought for several seconds, but when nothing came to me, I got up and walked down the steps to the grass. Roses and tuberoses perfumed the garden, their heady scent even more dense in the humid afternoon. I stretched out my arms, tilted my head back with my eyes closed, and inhabited the space. I got a little dizzy, but something told me that experiencing this position in this unfamiliar space was important, so I did it. I turned in a circle, then stopped and opened my eyes, facing Jezebel on the porch.

She gave a slight smile that urged me to explain what I was experiencing.

"When I was standing there with my eyes closed, I was trying to feel what the outside of me was like. I swear I felt the house—or you—over here, and the tree over there."

She nodded. "'Dat's close. 'De house has substance. 'De tree and I have life force. Could you tell 'de difference?"

"Not really." I rejoined her on the swing and slumped. "I'm starting to realize it's going to take forever to reach Mama."

Jezebel patted my leg. "Maybe you don't need to talk to her. Maybe she won't give you an answer anyway. Maybe it's up to you to decide how you gonna act. Grown-up or child? Practice meditation for a whole week, 'den come back and we talk some more."

Every time Jezebel dismissed me, the atmosphere changed, like she'd pulled down a curtain and blocked me out. It was no use trying to get more from her, so I said goodbye and headed home.

Chapter 22

Monday, August 26, 1974

"I'm jealous you get to put whatever you want out for however long you want. Your mama's things. Her picture. Her necklace. Even her rosary." Honey touched each item with appropriate reverence, then scanned the installation of new additions. "Mother makes me keep my dresser tidy, and only certain things can be there."

"That's her perfume too," I added. "Shalimar."

"Looks like an altar," Honey said.

Defensiveness welled up in my chest, but I knew she didn't mean anything by it.

"What's this?" Honey held up a purple stone, long and pointed at one end, held to a silver chain by a small silver cap. It was like a necklace, but it was too big and too long to be suitable for wearing around my neck.

"That's a pendulum. You ask it questions, and it starts to

move forward and back for yes, side to side for no. At least, that's what Jezebel said."

Honey dropped her hand at the mention of Jezebel's name. The stone clunked on the wooden dresser. "Why do you insist on listening to what that old woman says? Pendulums don't swing because you ask them questions and they give you answers. They swing because the earth rotates on its axis. Foucault proved it in 1851. Besides, if the pendulum was giving you answers, how do you know it isn't evil trying to sway you? God says only to listen to Him. Does He need a pendulum?" Honey set the offender back on my dresser and pushed it away from her.

Anytime I tried to listen to reason and science, even from Honey, I still had a gnawing feeling that there was something else to it. God had never spoken to me directly, only Mama, and that might not count because it was just her singing.

"Robert knows her, and he likes her."

Honey huffed. "That's not an answer."

She was right, but that's all I had. "Do you want to meditate with me?" I asked.

"What's meditate?"

"You relax and let your mind go blank. Then you observe whatever comes in."

Honey pursed her mouth. "You mean like spirits? I thought you learned a lesson with the Ouija board."

"Just Mama," I said. "I want to learn so I can talk to Mama."

Honey crossed her arms and shook her head. "No. I won't, and you shouldn't."

I tossed out a gem from Jezebel. "Praying is talking to God and praising Him. Meditation is listening."

"Where'd you hear that? And don't say Jezebel."

"Jezebel."

Honey rolled her eyes, then picked up the pendulum again. Mockingly, she said, "So if I asked it if it's really your mama talking to you, I'd get an answer?"

I egged her on by shrugging ever so slightly.

Honey held the pendulum by the chain and proceeded to ask if Mama was there. The pendulum started gently swinging back and forth. Honey dropped it onto the dresser like a sin and turned her back to it. "So . . . how's the wedding planning going?"

I laughed. "I try to avoid the subject with Miss Muriel because she starts talking like I'm actually interested, and then I'm stuck for an hour."

Honey scowled at me. "Why you are so mean to her?"

"I'm not mean. I'm just not . . . attached."

"If I were her, I'd be trying so hard for you to like me, and I think you'd be breaking my heart."

"She doesn't have a heart to break."

"Margaret Louise, you are out of your mind. Your daddy's found the nicest, most gentle . . . smartest lady in this whole parish. What's wrong with you? How can you say she doesn't have a heart?"

I expected Honey to take my side, but she was taking it less and less as Muriel burrowed more and more into my life.

Jezebel's words popped into my head. *You need three points to orient yourself.*

"Jezebel said—"

"I don't want to hear what that Voodoo Woman says, Margaret."

"Jezebel said," I continued, "that to know where you are, sometimes you need other points of perception to figure out if yours is right or wrong."

Honey tipped her head.

"And you and Daddy . . . heck, probably the whole darn town . . . think she's perfect. So why can't I see her that way? Why is my view so different from yours? What am I missing?"

"You're missing empathy and compassion."

"Ouch." I sulked and dropped onto the bed.

"You need to suck it up and stop being so whiny and wishy-washy about your daddy getting married. It's happening. Get over it."

Honey had never talked to me like that.

"I'm not wishy-washy." I stood and stomped out of the room, knowing Honey would follow me and apologize because she hated conflict even more than I did.

I walked halfway down the block before I stopped listening for footsteps behind me. I didn't even know where I was going. By the time I circled the block and came home, Honey was gone. She'd left a note on my dresser.

Bye. See you tomorrow. Don't be mad.

Chapter 23

Wednesday, August 28, 1974

My anger walk two days ago showed me that it actually helped me think and organize my thoughts, so today, I wandered around the neighborhood, not on the way to anywhere, just thinking about everything Jezebel had said the last time I was with her.

It was a little overwhelming. I still couldn't tell if I was making things up or getting information from spirit when I meditated.

A little past ten, I found myself at Jezebel's like I found myself at school most days: not remembering the walk because I was deep in thought and the route was so familiar. I knocked on the front door; the floorboards creaked as Jezebel moved across them. When she opened the door, the smell of bacon and eggs invited me in.

"I'm sorry," I said. "I didn't think you'd be eating. I'll come back later."

"'Dat's alright, baby. Come in. You can eat too, or not."

Jezebel didn't leave room for argument.

I sat at the dinette in the kitchen and she brought me tea.

"You want eggs and bacon?"

"No, ma'am. I already had some this morning. May I have a piece of toast, though? I love the grape jam you have."

"Of course you can."

She popped two slices into the toaster and waited for them to brown. Jezebel wasn't the mother type, but she gave off the vibe as she spooned jam into a tiny bowl for me. She set it and a small plate in front of me. When the toast was ready, she carried both pieces over and gave me mine, then said a prayer over our food.

I already had my question of the day prepared, but first the sweet and crunchy combination of toast and jam. After savoring a couple bites, I said, "Jezebel, why don't I ever see Mama? I know she's near me. I hear her and feel her and smell her, but I've never seen anything."

Jezebel pointed a finger downward. "Close your eyes and look at your feet."

I scooted out from the table and closed my eyes. I remembered putting on my Chuck Taylors this morning, but for some strange reason, I was barefoot. "Huh."

"What you see?" Jezebel asked.

"I don't see anything, but I feel like I'm barefoot."

"So, don't most people wear shoes?"

"Yeah, I guess so."

I wasn't understanding where this was going.

"So why aren't you?" Jezebel demanded.

"Because I'm not?"

I opened my eyes. Jezebel was grinning at me. "Close your eyes again and go to 'de side yard and get me a chicken."

"How am I supposed to do that if I'm sitting here with my eyes closed and I can't see anything? I didn't know you had chickens."

"You'll figure it out." She waved her hand in dismissal and I closed my eyes again.

I let frustration cloud my thinking for a few moments but pushed it aside. In my imagination, I walked around the side of the house, and as I got near a coop that didn't exist in the real world, I called out, "Hey, chicken, will you go with me to see Jezebel?"

"Sure," a chicken answered and hopped on my outstretched left arm.

I walked back to the kitchen in triumph with the imaginary chicken on my arm; its talons were sharp on my skin, and its weight shifted as I walked.

When I opened my eyes, Jezebel's grin was even bigger.

"I think I get it," I said. "It's not *how* I get information; it's that I *get* information."

Jezebel leaned forward. "'Dat's right."

"But how do I know it's information from spirit and not my imagination?"

"Ah, good questions from you, Miss Margaret." She took another bite of eggs and bacon and chewed it slowly, then took a long sip of tea. "Close your eyes. Imagine a couch wit' a blue cushion. You see it?"

"No, but I know it's there. I don't know how to describe it."

"Good enough. Now make 'de cushion color change to green. Got it?"

"Yes, it's green now."

"Now yellow. Now red. When you can change information, whe'der you see it, feel it, or know it, 'dat's your imagination. You direct your brain what to 'tink." Jezebel stopped speaking, and I opened my eyes again. "'De difference between imagination and spirit is like 'de difference between speaking and singing. 'Dey come from 'de same place, but you use your physicality, your body, in ano'der way."

"I still don't get how I'd know the difference." I took another bite of toast. "I can taste color, you know."

"You can? Well, 'dat's interesting. What does 'de red cushion taste like?"

I concentrated on red. "Peanuts."

"Blue cushion?"

"Mmm . . . salmon."

"Huh. 'Dis happen all 'de time?"

"No ma'am. Only if I really concentrate on a color or a taste. They kind of overlap."

"'Dat would be distracting. No wonder you all over 'de place."

"I kind of like it," I said, a tiny bit defensive.

"Hm." Jezebel surveyed me for a moment. "Anyway, next time you hear your mama, try to change 'de song she sings or how her perfume smells. You might be able to change it for a split second, but if it's her, it will change right back because it isn't your mind directing 'de information. Maybe for you, it's different, but 'de lwa, 'de spirits, give me information by energy touching parts of my brain. 'Dey touch like a menu in my brain to get me to say, or feel, or see some'ting. 'Dis why people get different information from spirits, because 'de people's brains are different and 'dat's what spirit uses to communicate. Like I said, complicated."

"Okay, I think I get the idea." I finished the rest of my toast, then asked, "So, when you talk to the lwa, how do you do it?"

"'Dat's ano'der big question. You ever ask any little questions?"

"Asking big questions is my forte."

Jezebel got up to put more hot water in her tea. "Before you can learn to talk wit' 'de spirits, you need to learn to manage energy. 'Dat's another 'ting meditation helps wit'. Two ways to deal wit' energy—close it off or learn to manage it. I spent much of my life pleasing o'ders because it made 'dere energy more easier to be around. You do 'dat?"

"I never thought of it that way. I'm a rule follower. I won't cross the street unless the light is green, and I always return the carts at the grocery store. Daddy is much easier to be around when I follow his rules too. So, I guess I do. Is it bad?"

"No, not so much when you're young, but as you get older, you don't want everyone pushing you around. You have to manage 'de energy a bit."

"What does that mean, to 'manage the energy'? Like, manipulate people?"

"No, I mean manage 'de energy as it comes to you. Make

it so good energy comes in easy, and bad energy doesn't come in at all. You can't control what o'der people's energy is like, how it comes into you. 'Tink of 'de difference of being in church to being in 'de school cafeteria. Church is usually good energy, people on 'de same page, nice and calm. Cafeteria, wit' all 'dose hormonal boys and girls . . . crazy, scattered energy. So, you don't go 'dere if you don't like 'de energy, but you can learn to not let it affect you so much."

"It's something I learn how to do for me, not to do to someone else?"

"'Dat's right again."

"Honey said the pendulum you gave me doesn't move because of spirits. It moves because the earth moves."

"She's right about 'de earth moving. But I'm right about spirit influencing your body to move wid'out you being aware of it."

Jezebel had told me so many things that it was getting difficult to remember it all.

"Your friend doesn't like me much, no?"

"Oh, no. I mean—she doesn't know you." Jezebel's detection of Honey's attitude surprised me. "She's really nice. You'd like her."

"What's not to like about Honey?"

It was a rhetorical question.

Chapter 24

Saturday, August 31, 1974

Muriel arrived to have breakfast with Daddy as I was cutting up strawberries to top my giant bowl of Cheerios, whole milk, and sugar cubes. She kissed me on the cheek as she passed by. I wiped it with my shoulder.

"Thank you for making coffee," Muriel said. "It's so thoughtful of you."

"Oh, you're welcome. Hope it's not too strong. Daddy likes it strong."

"Your daddy likes everything strong. It's what makes him love you so much."

"He loves me because I make strong coffee?"

"No, silly. You are strong."

I stared at her and she laughed, a sweet, melodious sound that drifted and hung in the air.

"Thanks," I mumbled.

"I want to thank you too, Margaret, for being so nice and

welcoming to me. I know it's probably been hard for you, accepting a new mother. I'm here *for* you, not against you. Whenever you need me."

She said the words I didn't want to accept: "new mother." If she was just going to be Daddy's wife, maybe I could live with it. But that wasn't her intent. She intended to be my mother. She wasn't, and I wouldn't let her become it. I needed something to make her go away. Daddy already laid down the law on disruptive behavior, so that was a long shot.

I finished my breakfast offering no further chitchat, wondering if Jezebel had some potion or a spell that would make Muriel disappear, then excused myself and dashed out the back door.

The morning rain was musical on the roof as I stood on Jezebel's porch and knocked. When she answered, she hesitated before opening the door wider, making me wonder if I had come at a bad time, but she invited me in. I sat on the ugly couch, and she settled in the rocker.

"I need your help," I said. "I know you're giving me all this information, and I appreciate it, I really do, but I don't know how long it'll take me to learn it all so I can talk to Mama and ask her if I should let Daddy and Miss Muriel get married."

"Let 'dem?"

"Well, yes. I guess I haven't told you why I want to talk to Mama so bad. Daddy's going to marry Muriel Lafleur, Dr. Lafleur. Do you know her?"

Jezebel rocked slowly and nodded.

"And we, Honey and I, we found poems on Mama's grave that Daddy didn't write, and I want to know what it means, and I want to be able to have Mama close all the time, and Daddy won't talk about her, and I miss her. It feels like I'm betraying her if I approve of Daddy getting married. That's why I need to talk to her." I was frantic to get all my reasons out, to convince Jezebel to use her knowledge of Vodou. "Is there a potion or spell that will let me? My second option is to make Muriel go away. Is there a potion for that? That might be easier. She would disappear, and things would go back to how they were."

Jezebel continued rocking with a steady gaze on me. My cheeks grew hot.

"First, I told you, you can't make anyone do any'ting. Next, after all I taught you, you still want a magic spell to solve your problem?"

I swallowed hard and nodded, intimidated more by the slight old woman in front of me than by anyone else in my life.

Jezebel got up and walked into the kitchen. She pulled something off a shelf and flipped pages back and forth. She made grunting noises too. When she came back to the living room, she had turned sullen and wouldn't look at me. She handed me a slip of paper with a recipe written in a halting script.

"It only works during a full moon," she said. "Tomorrow. It won't work on angels."

With that I got the cue to leave.

I didn't like Jezebel's scowl of disappointment, but I reasoned that she didn't understand my position. I couldn't spend weeks learning how to do all she taught me. I needed answers and guidance now.

The potion was sickening on paper: tomato juice, cayenne pepper, paprika, beets, nutmeg, cinnamon, and dill. Half the battle would be making it; the other half would be getting Muriel to drink it.

Muriel had a ladies tea at our house tomorrow afternoon with The Fish from her church. It would be easy to give her the drink in front of them. Her manners would not permit her to refuse. I could get The Fish to drink it too.

If I'd made something as dangerous as nitroglycerine with Robert, surely I could handle a disappearing potion.

When I finished my chores, I went up to my room to meditate. I lay down on my bed, leaving the candles unlit, and stared at the diamonds of light that shone on the ceiling from the window glass. It was a dangerous position, as easy to fall asleep as to meditate, but I was willing to risk it.

I was soon on the familiar yet unknown beach. This time, I could feel my hands touching the warm sand and the sensation of movement when I held them up and the sand escaped through my fingers.

Again, Muriel showed up on the beach, but instead of objecting and ruining the meditation, I let her go to see what would happen. Muriel tipped her hat to me but stayed near the water's edge, bending to pick up a shell and letting her toes get overrun with the wavelets that glided over the sand.

She was unobtrusive but glanced back at me often. No suspicion, no malice in her movement. It was like she was watching over me but didn't want me to know.

A knock on the bedroom door woke me up. "We're leaving for dinner now," Daddy said. "Miss Muriel put a plate of leftovers in the icebox for you."

"Thank you," I called out, then remembered to add, "Have fun."

I made the potion in a pretty glass pitcher, one I remembered Mama serving me lemonade from when it was sultry outside, with a white linen napkin wrapped near the top to catch spills. After adding all the ingredients, I stirred the mixture until it looked like the drink it pretended to be, then placed a celery stalk with the leaves on it into the mix. I dipped my finger in and tasted it. Even the smallest drop proved it was a pungent, tangy concoction. I opened the icebox and moved the plate of food. I could take care of myself, thank you.

Robert knocked on the back door and let himself in as he usually did if Daddy wasn't home. He nodded toward the pitcher. "Whacha makin'?"

I stammered and set it on the counter. Guilt crept up like a blush of embarrassment as I distanced myself from it.

"Oh, this? It's nothing."

"Is it a pitcher of Bloody Mary?"

"Yes . . . that's what it is. For Miss Muriel's tea tomorrow."

"Look at you, knowing how to make Bloody Mary. I guess I'm not the only one who can make something to get us in trouble." Robert laughed at his own joke and searched the cupboard for a glass.

"Oh, no. You're not going to try it."

"Why not? I've had one before."

I panicked and snatched it off the counter, then placed it front and center in the icebox so Muriel would know I'd made it for her ladies tea. I slammed the door and threw my back against it. "I'll make us some popcorn, and we can watch TV." The offer was enough to distract Robert. "Let's call Honey too," I added.

Just as the popcorn fell into the bowl, Honey arrived.

I don't remember what we watched, but it kept Robert and Honey interested while I imagined ways I would offer the potion to Muriel.

That night, I had a dream that Muriel was lost at sea and Daddy was away searching for her. Honey and Robert, and even Jezebel, wagged their fingers at me, but I couldn't hear the accusations they made, only a roaring sound that turned out to be rain against the window and a tree branch stuck on the roof, rasping against the shingles.

Chapter 25

Sunday, September 1, 1974

I woke up exhausted, dread in my chest like I'd done something terrible to cause last night's dreams. Or had I done something terrible in the dream? A rock in my gut weighed me down. I ran down the stairs, ready to pour the potion down the sink. It wasn't worth the risk.

I opened the icebox to retrieve the Bloody Mary potion, and a space yawned where it should have been. My heart pounded and my pulse jumped in my neck, distracting me and making it hard to concentrate.

"Margaret?"

I jumped. It was Muriel. She came around the corner, an empty glass in her hand.

"Did you make that pitcher of Bloody Mary in the icebox?" she asked. "I appreciate you trying to make something for the ladies tea, but it's . . . not so good." Before I could respond, she added, "Perhaps you can help me make sweet tea instead."

With more fear in my voice than concern, I asked, "Are you okay?"

Her hand fluttered up to her forehead. "I don't feel well."

"Umm . . ." I pulled out a kitchen chair. "Maybe you should sit down."

As Muriel moved toward the chair, she slumped to the floor, as graceful a fall as I'd ever seen. The glass didn't even break.

"Muriel!" I rushed over and shook her shoulder. "I'm sorry. I didn't mean it. Please don't disappear."

I couldn't see anything through the tears in my eyes. Muriel lay still for a moment and then shivered violently. After several seconds she stopped and opened her eyes. She was motionless at first, then she burst out laughing. I sat back hard on the floor as Muriel pushed herself up to a sitting position. She covered her mouth with both hands, but her squeals escaped anyway.

"You faked fainting?" I stood and crossed my arms. "How could you? That scared me so bad."

"Well," she said, unable to contain her grin, "you did try to make me disappear."

How did she know?

Muriel got up and took me by the shoulders, squaring me so we were face to face. Her voice sounded far away. "Margaret, that potion doesn't work on me."

I froze, remembering Jezebel's strange and offhand remark: *It won't work on angels.* I took in a breath, unsure how to respond. But instead of pressing me on it, Muriel thanked me in advance for making the tea, then returned to the living room to finish preparing the space for her guests as if nothing had happened.

I got the tea ready and bolted out the back door. It was still early on Sunday, but I banged on Jezebel's door with teenage insistence, not caring if I woke her from a lazy morning sleep.

The second she opened the door, I blurted out, "You tricked me!"

"I did no such 'ting." She opened the door wide. "Good morning, Miss Margaret."

I shirked my manners, pushing into the living room like I owned the place. "You said it would make her disappear. Well, it didn't. She drank a whole glass. And then, and *then*, she said, 'That doesn't work on me,' as if she was an angel. She's no angel. How did she know to say that? Did you tell her? Did you?"

Jezebel brought her hand to her mouth, trying to keep a straight face. "I never said it would make her disappear. You said 'dat."

"Then what was the potion for?"

"No potion. Bloody Mary wit' a few gross 'tings put in. Enough for you to believe."

My tone pitched higher. "Why did you give me something fake?"

"Because I was trying to give you some'ting real 'de last few weeks and you weren't having it. You want 'de magic pill, 'de magic potion, to make your life go back to 'de way it was. Life's not like 'dat, but you don't listen to old Jezebel."

I sat down hard on the couch and crossed my arms.

Jezebel strode into the kitchen. After a few minutes, the water hissed, timid at first and then insistent until she lifted the kettle off the flame. She brought a tray with tea and some biscuits to the coffee table, serving me as if we hadn't just been yelling at each other.

"Your judgment got clouded about lots of 'tings." She handed me my cup. "Maybe now you see you have to do 'de work to get to 'de answers. What you 'tink of Miss Muriel now?"

I stared into the brew. "I don't know what to think."

Jezebel sat back in the rocker, her eyes on me.

"I guess I've been so busy asking everyone else what they think, and what *I* should think about Muriel . . . I don't know if I have an opinion about her, just her, at all."

I scanned the books and knickknacks in the room, stopping on a pink rock, exactly like the one Muriel put in the dining room, sitting on a shelf behind Jezebel. I set my tea down and walked over to the stone. "What's this?"

Jezebel twisted around. "Rose quartz, a crystal. Bring it here. I'll show you."

It filled my palm and weighed it down. I sat on the floor at Jezebel's feet.

"Rose quartz has 'de meanings of love—all kinds of love—romantic, mo'derly, friendship. And it's pretty."

"Miss Muriel put one of these in our dining room. I thought it was just a rock."

"Oh, no, it's much more 'dan 'dat. Miss Muriel, she knows when a place needs a boost of love."

"My house has plenty of love, thank you."

"Don't get huffy. I didn't say it didn't. But anywhere can have more love, right? How is more love bad?"

She had me there, but still. "How do you know Muriel would know what this rock means?"

"Crystal, not rock," she corrected. "Because I told her."

I jumped up. "What?"

"You're so jumpy. Jump to conclusions, jump to anger. Sit down. Over 'dere." Jezebel pointed to the couch. "You 'tink because I say no one comes here anymore 'dat no one ever did? No, baby, I know most people in 'dis town. And 'de next few towns too. Miss Muriel, I've known her since before she was a doctor."

I couldn't believe what I was hearing. "You mean . . . I could have asked you if I could trust her?"

"Yes."

My mind spun. "Jezebel?"

"What, baby?"

"Did you know my mama?"

Jezebel smiled. "Oh, yes, Miss Veone."

I swallowed hard. "Do you . . . do you know why she took the sleeping pills? I mean, do you know if it was an accident or on purpose?"

Jezebel stopped rocking and leaned toward me. "Is 'dat ano'der reason you want to talk to her so bad?"

My heart swelled. "Yes, I mean . . . I guess it doesn't make a difference, but it matters to me. Even though it doesn't seem like it matters to anyone else."

She started rocking again and looked at me tenderly. "Why don't you ask your daddy? He knows."

Chapter 26

Friday, September 6, 1974

Hurricane Carmen was in the Gulf, headed straight for Louisiana. She'd formed over a week ago, but that far out, no one knew where she was headed until a few days before landfall. On Friday, she was a Category Two, but by early Sunday morning, she was expected to hit us as a Category Three. I didn't know what that meant exactly, but Daddy seemed concerned.

"School's supposed to start next week," I said as we finished supper. "And it hasn't been summer at all."

Daddy set his plate in the sink and took mine. "It's been hot as Hades, and you've had a few adventures. What hasn't been like summer?"

I shrugged. "I haven't been as lazy as I planned . . . you know, reading books, fishing. Life's been too busy, and now this hurricane might mess it up even more."

It hadn't been summer because I hadn't made any progress

in contacting Mama, and now I was even more confused about Muriel.

After doing the dishes together, we went outside. The wind was still mild—the best time to put up the shutters. Placing the ladder against the house, Daddy said, "You can invite Honey and Robert to stay over if you want for a hurricane party."

"I asked them already," I said, climbing up to inspect the windows and confirm the hooks were in place for the Bahama shutters to hinge on. "They both have to stay home."

Daddy stood with his foot bracing the ladder. "Oh. Okay, then."

"Is this gonna be a big storm?"

"So they say."

I looked down with a shudder. "I wish there was a way to hang these without being way up here!" The higher I climbed, the thinner my voice came out, so I had to yell at this point.

"Just don't look down. You're doing fine."

I'd started helping Daddy the summer after Mama died. The shutters were still too heavy for me to hang by myself, so my job was to inspect the windows. Some folks left their shutters up all year so they didn't have to put them up if a storm was coming, but Daddy said it made the house too dark, so he preferred to set them on their hinges when needed. He had them made in smaller panels so they were more easily portable, but still they were heavy and cumbersome, especially the ones for the second floor, and I feared more than once that Daddy would fall during the operation. Thankfully, he never did.

The air carried that just-before-lightning scent. As I climbed down, the electric particles in the sky made my mouth taste like metal.

"I'm kinda worried about this one," Daddy said. "I think we'll be fine, but it might get a bit scary."

I loved lightning, thunder, wind, and rain, so the prospect of a hurricane wasn't scary, it was exciting. "We'll be okay," I assured him, stepping off the last rung. "The windows are ready."

After Daddy finished hanging the shutters and put all the tools away, we gathered flashlights, water, and food and put them upstairs in the master closet, a space with no outside doors or windows should the storm get wicked. It wasn't a big room, but we made it comfortable by laying pillows and blankets on the orange and brown shag, which hadn't been replaced when the upstairs was re-carpeted after Mama died.

The last big storm to hit the area was when I was five, so I didn't remember much. Louisiana tended to get them every few years, so we stayed in practice with storm preparation and kept supplies on hand that would get us through three days or so. The power went out often with regular storms, so it was likely it would be the same with this one.

I followed Daddy down the stairs, our preparations for Carmen complete.

"Daddy, is Miss Muriel going to be staying at St. Joseph's?"

"Yep. In case she's needed, she didn't want to have to

drive to the hospital during the storm. It's a safe place to be . . . and she'll admit patients to the hospital if necessary."

I paused. "What if . . . something happens to her?"

Daddy wheeled around, his face right at mine. "Why would you say that?"

"I don't know, just asking."

Daddy braced the railing and leaned in to his words. "Nothing's going to happen to any of us. I swear, sometimes you are so negative. Why do you always think something bad is going to happen?"

"Because bad things *do* happen. To you, to me, to everyone. I'd rather have it in my mind than be blindsided."

"I'd rather deal with what actually happens than worry about all kinds of stuff that won't."

"Is that the war talking?"

Daddy continued toward the kitchen. "Maybe."

"But we put up shutters and make sure the roof is in good shape in case something happens."

"That's different. We know a hurricane's coming."

He was right. Something *was* coming. I wasn't sure if it was the hurricane or something else, but the rock in my gut, the one I first sensed when I woke up from the dream of Muriel lost at sea, was so disquieting that I squirmed to detach it. I'd never felt anything like it before, and I couldn't wait to ask Jezebel what it meant.

Chapter 27

Sunday, September 8, 1974

We didn't get much sleep, not even in our own beds. The wind and rain started near midnight, and by 4:00 a.m., the power went out and we couldn't ignore the sound.

We both got up for breakfast at the same time. The wind moaned, followed by whistles and clunks as things skidded down the street or hit the house. The sun rose somewhere, but the storm blocked nine-tenths of it. Daddy tried reading, pacing, and reading again, but being in a storm with nothing to take your mind off it was distressing. I tried a crossword puzzle after a breakfast of cereal and milk, which Daddy had too, so the milk wouldn't go bad when the power went out.

Thibodaux would be on the east side of the storm once it came ashore. West is the best, and east is a beast, or so the saying goes, which meant we would be in the beast.

I expected that being in a hurricane would be like sitting in my room when it rained; the soft and persistent tapping could lull me to sleep or let me disappear into a story. But the hurricane was different. It insisted that you pay attention. Its sounds made your heart race, and it poured rain like someone dumping a bucket on the house. Worst of all, I couldn't see out. The shutters were closed tight, so our imaginations dictated what the world looked like outside. With no TV to give us updates, we had no idea how long we'd be captive—or safe—in our own home.

The wind was ramping up as Daddy and I sat in the kitchen, beginning a game of Go Fish with the howl at octaves I'd never heard before, when he said it was time to go to the closet to be safe.

We resumed our game upstairs, but instead of asking if he had any twos or sevens, I said, "Daddy, I need to ... know some things about Mama."

The gusts were so loud that we had to fit words in between them.

"I'm so glad we changed the wedding date from yesterday," he said.

I wasn't sure if he hadn't heard me or was deflecting. Either way, the raucous flailing outside outside only strengthened my resolve. "We're talking about this, Daddy. Now. Today. Hurricane or not. Did Mama kill herself?"

Daddy was taken aback. He looked at the floor as the noise outside rose and fell.

"I don't think so," he finally said.

I waited for him to go on, to fill in the blanks he must have known existed in my head. But he said nothing.

"Why did she have the sleeping pills in the first place?" I pushed.

The wind roared, then quieted.

"She wasn't sleeping, so the doctor gave her some."

"Why couldn't she sleep?"

"I don't know."

The tightness in my throat nearly strangled me as I waited for another lull.

"Honey and I found poetry on her grave. Someone loved her and misses her."

Daddy suddenly got up and threw the closet door open. I followed him as he clomped down the stairs and into the kitchen. He leaned against the white Formica counter. Tears flowed down his cheeks.

The hot sting of regret filled my face. I'd never seen him cry, not after the funeral or in the days following, and certainly not since then.

"I'm sorry," I said. "I didn't mean it."

He started making choking sounds, then slid to the floor like a little boy. I'd never seen him lose it like this.

"She wasn't having an affair," he said to the floor.

I sat down gently across from him. "What's an affair?"

"She didn't—she wasn't—in love with someone else."

I kept my voice low. "Then what are the poems? Who wrote them? What do they mean?"

Daddy sighed and wiped his face with his hand. "I put them there."

"You did? But it isn't your handwriting."

"Old man Merriweather."

"What does he have to do with it?"

"He writes poetry."

I shook my head. "Still not making sense."

Daddy leaned his head against the cabinet and stared up at the ceiling. "He writes poetry, and he throws out poetry. Drafts. One time, a piece of one came out of the garbage bag and landed at my feet. I read it, and it reminded me of your mama, so I took it to her. I could never write anything decent, so using someone else's words made me happy. So, I did it again . . . this time, I looked for something to express what I wanted to say. I didn't consider that anyone would ever see them before they blew away or got ruined by the rain." He wiped his face again. "They weren't from someone else. If that's what's made you act up, I'm sorry. It was innocent."

I reached out and touched his arm, forgiving him for unknowingly putting me through torture.

"Then why, Daddy? Why did she have sleeping pills?"

The wind rose with intensity and stayed loud. When a lull finally came, he said, "She had a miscarriage."

The words hit me like a slap. Never in my life had anyone said anything about a baby. My mind raced to memories of Mama. She was never big-bellied in any of them.

"I don't remember her pregnant," I said.

Daddy sighed again. "Sixteen weeks. Daniel Tracy. He wasn't very big yet."

"Oh," I said softly.

"The doctor at the hospital promised to let us bury him, but she kept saying she couldn't do it . . . so I put him with her in the coffin."

The wind screamed outside. "Why didn't you tell me?"

Before Daddy could answer, a crashing sound outside sent us hustling upstairs. Back inside the closet, Daddy sat in a corner, as far away from me as he could. The nest we'd built provided protection from the storm, but we couldn't escape each other.

"Why Miss Muriel?" I badgered.

"Why not Miss Muriel? I have no earthly idea why you dislike her so."

"She's not Mama."

Daddy shook his head and looked away. The wind continued to howl in a rising and falling pitch.

"You put her things away, you won't talk about her, and you brought Miss Muriel into our family. She'll never be gone for me. I just want to have her be part of my life still."

Daddy returned his eyes to mine. "Why can't you do that? What's stopping you? She's in your heart."

"Oh, Daddy, that's so trite. *You* are stopping me. Muriel is. Honey, Robert. Everyone."

Daddy took in a breath. "Margaret, when someone dies, they are gone. You can't talk to them or see them or feel them. It's all in your imagination. I know you miss her, but thinking you can keep her with you is just . . . it's not . . ."

It was rare for him to not finish a sentence.

"It's not what?"

"It's not . . . normal."

Daddy's accusation hung in the air like Muriel's laughter. He kept talking, but I crossed my arms and tried to shut him out.

"As long as you are under my roof—"

"You will follow my rules," I interrupted. "I know. What rule am I breaking now?"

"Tone of voice at the moment."

The rain beat against the roof in shooshing waves, carried by the equally fierce wind.

I tried to call Mama close, to bring her to me, but she was very far away, and this time, I couldn't blame Muriel.

"Daddy, what if you, just once, believed that I can feel and hear Mama? Why wouldn't you want to know that? To feel her too?"

"I did feel her once, in a dream. It was very real."

"What?" I shouted. "So, you know this isn't bullshit?"

Daddy closed his eyes briefly and kept his voice steady. "It was just a dream."

"Maybe it wasn't. Maybe we can still communicate. Maybe we aren't separated from them at all."

Daddy shifted uncomfortably. "I'm never talking about this again, Margaret. Miss Muriel and I are getting married, and I don't want to live in the past."

"Mama's not my past. I want to talk about her all the time."

"Well, I don't."

"Oh, so, since it's your house and your rules, I just have to give up ever thinking about my Mama? Just poof—she never existed?" I was exaggerating but kept on, eager to bury him under guilt and remorse.

"I couldn't have loved her any more than I did. But sometimes . . . it's not enough."

He wrapped his arms around his knees. Protection. From me. I didn't need to bury him under guilt and remorse. He'd done it to himself long ago.

"I can't go forward with her. I need to leave her behind. I need to abandon that part of my life to build a new one. I know not everyone does, but I do. She didn't abandon *you*, though."

"What? Where'd that come from? I never said that."

"What I mean is, she wouldn't have left you on purpose."

"Of course she wouldn't. She loved me. She loves me."

"Miss Muriel won't abandon you either."

Fear rose in my chest that she'd told Daddy what I'd done with the potion. I'd tried to make her disappear in my frantic desire to be rid of this unwanted situation. It was ludicrous to think a potion would make someone disappear, but I'd wanted it so badly that I believed it when I thought it up—and Jezebel had done nothing to dissuade me.

Daddy continued. "I think you must fear someone leaving you since Mama died, but it's only a fear. You don't deserve it. You didn't make it happen. It's just a fear."

I didn't agree, but I let him ascribe his thought to my actions as a way of explanation. I tipped my head against the wall and felt the tremor of the wind send primal vibrations through me.

Chapter 28

Monday, September 9, 1974

I heard Daddy on the roof at first light, taking down the shutters. I didn't bother to get up to help him. When he removed the ones from my window, he peeked in and smiled at me.

It was amazing how the wild, screaming wind of yesterday had morphed into the calm and quiet demeanor of today. It had left a stark aftermath in its wake, though. Leaves and branches littered the ground. No birds sang. Water languished in puddles everywhere, and I could see that power poles now tilted a few degrees.

Honey, Robert, and I set off to explore and walked the neighborhood to survey the damage. Daddy even asked for me to report back, all official like. The neighborhood smelled clean, like the storm had carried away any rot. I'd thought it would smell the opposite. Still, they delayed the start of school for two weeks for the town to clean up.

"Looks like power lines, gardens, and shingle damage," Robert said as we all leapt over a giant puddle in the middle of Legard Street.

"It sure sounded like more things should be out of place," I added. "Daddy said the radio reported the tide came up six feet. Let's go look at the bayou."

At the Talking Tree, the grass squished under our feet, and we sank up to our ankles. Robert and I enjoyed making a mess in the mud. We splashed around for a while and then the three of us took the footbridge that led to the sugarcane fields north of town. The canes had already grown to nine feet when Hurricane Carmen pushed them down like a bully, and now parts of the field lay flat, like they'd been harvested already. Luckily, cane was resilient, so the harvesters would still get something out of the crop.

By the time we circled around to see the damage to the buildings and old homes downtown, the sun was blazing and no breeze moved through the streets. Shingles littered the road, and power poles were tilted here too. The whole town still lacked power, so we didn't worry about getting electrocuted by downed lines.

The muddy water sloshed as cars drove through it. One of the cars was David's Mustang. As he passed, he sped up to splash us, then laughed with his friends.

"What an asshole," Robert said. It was what we all were thinking, though in my head I added "cute asshole."

After David was out of sight, I said, "Let's go see if Jezebel's okay."

Robert agreed, but Honey didn't want to go.

I tugged on her arm. "Aw, come on. You'll like her, I swear."

But Honey insisted on going home. She lacked her usual energy, though, and didn't even lecture us about voodoo being bad.

"I have to go to Mass anyway if they have it," she said. "I'll see you guys tomorrow."

As Honey walked away, Robert said, "You think she's okay? She seems off."

I pulled up the times Honey had ever seemed off and sifted through them, not finding any that matched today's "off."

"Yeah. It's not like her. I'll talk to her later."

We turned toward Jezebel's and picked our way through the littered streets. We found a teddy bear, wet and ruined; a single high-heeled shoe, pink satin with a bow on top; and a man's fancy wristwatch. Robert picked the watch up and looked around, as if trying to place where it came from.

"This is all stuff from inside someone's house. Somebody must have had a lot of damage."

I nodded but didn't want us getting derailed. "Let's take it to Jezebel. She might know how to find the owner."

Robert brightened at the idea. Though it wasn't his responsibility to return any of our finds, his honest and caring nature made him want to. At times, he was a bit *too* responsible and honest.

"It's going to take some work to get things back to the way they used to be," he said, "but everyone was pretty lucky."

Just then, a thought came from outside my head. It wasn't

words or pictures. It was an idea, fully formed and understood. I grabbed Robert's arm and stopped walking.

"Mama dying was like a hurricane going through my life. I need to rebuild, but I can't leave the destruction, like leaves and branches in the road. I just don't know what pieces to put back where they belong, which ones to send to the dump, and which ones to build all over again . . . like with new materials, hard work, and a coat of paint. It won't ever be the same, but sometime in the future, I'll hardly remember there was ever a storm."

"That's deep," Robert said. "Are you talking about your Daddy getting married?"

We resumed walking. "Kind of. Daddy and I had it out during the storm. I told him I just want Mama to be part of my life still."

Robert rubbed his chin. "Seems to me you've already been doing that. Maybe not in the way everyone likes, but you've been working on it."

I stood up straight and smiled. "You think so? That makes me feel so much better. I felt like I was getting ripped apart yesterday, and now everything is so calm."

"You talk about her all the time. Isn't that keeping her close?"

"Yeah, I guess so."

"And you have some of her things. That's her wedding ring, isn't it?" Robert pointed to my pinky. "Jezebel is helping too." He said it as a statement, not a question.

When we reached Jezebel's house, she was standing on

her front porch, surveying the damage from a safe vantage point. She motioned us up to the house.

"*Mon Dieu*, but 'dat was a storm, no?"

"You should see the sugarcane fields," I said. "They're all messed up."

"I bet 'dey are." She waved her hand. "You two come in."

I'd never been at her house with anyone else. Robert chose to sit in the ladder-back cane chair—the one that matched ours. Since Mama's funeral, I'd never sat in it again, nor had I sat in Jezebel's, but Robert looked comfortable in it, like he'd sat there many times before.

Jezebel brought us some water.

"Thank you," Robert said. "We came to check on you. Looks like you're doing fine."

"I am. You're both so nice to come see me. How did you all make out?"

"We found this watch in the street. Do you know who it might belong to?"

Jezebel took it and examined the back for an inscription. "No idea. You like me to take it to 'de police? Looks like it may be expensive."

Robert nodded. "Yes, ma'am. Please."

"Daddy and I had a fight during the storm," I said, jumping in to answer her original question. "When we left earlier to see what damage was done, he asked for a report when I got back, so he must not be too mad still."

Jezebel leaned forward in her rocker and squinted. "What you say to him to make him mad?"

"How do you know it was something I said?"

Robert chuckled. "It's always something you say."

I abruptly changed the subject.

"The damage around town isn't too bad."

Jezebel smiled wryly. "No'ting hard work and a coat of paint won't fix, no?"

Chapter 29

Tuesday, September 10, 1974

Daddy was already asleep for the night as I lit the candles in my room. I'd taken some from the sideboard in the dining room to add to my Piggly Wiggly one, along with a few taller tapers Daddy would never miss. Better to ask forgiveness than permission, so I didn't tell him what I was doing.

Jezebel said to start by centering myself through breathing. I didn't know what she meant by "centered," but I drew in the scent of vanilla rose with a deep and cleansing breath, then another. "Centered" seemed like the right adjective. Meditation was getting easier.

"Mar-gar-et!" Robert called. "Hey! Come to the window!"

My eyes popped open. Robert sometimes made it impossible for me to sit by myself and think on summer nights.

My bedroom was conveniently over the roof of the wraparound porch, and I'd started crawling out there when I was ten. He'd open his window, I'd climb out and around to his side, and we would talk back and forth.

I opened the screen, and leaned far out. "What do you want, Rob-ert?" I answered, mimicking his forced whisper.

"Can you come over?"

"No, it's too late."

"How about sitting out on the roof?"

"Okay." A warm gulf breeze fluttered the curtains as I stepped out. I scooted to the right side of the house, where we were only about ten feet apart, and settled back against the siding.

I waited for him to start, but he sat like a lump with his head down. The streetlight backlit him and I couldn't see his features clearly, but it illuminated mine. I made a face at him, trying to lighten the mood, but he didn't raise his head.

"What's up?" I finally asked.

"Have you ever liked anyone? You know, *liked* them?"

"No," I lied.

"Oh. Well, do you and Honey ever talk about liking someone?"

A nervous laugh escaped. "Not really." I worried he was thinking about the day he caught me staring at David. "Well, sometimes maybe, but nothing serious, just teasing each other."

"Oh. Does Honey like anyone?"

My legs itched against the asphalt shingles and I crossed them. Robert sat still in the darkness.

When I didn't answer, he said, "Well, I like her."

The pronouncement was so shocking to me, it barely registered. The world fell away, and I got the distinct sense I'd just heard a secret that would change all our lives.

He raised his head. "She's the perfect girl. Besides you, I mean." He was considerate to a fault.

I swallowed hard. "She is." I fiddled with a leaf. "Why don't you tell her?"

"I'm afraid, I guess."

"Afraid of what?"

"You know, all the things you can be afraid of. That she doesn't like me back . . . or that she does." He shifted his position and leaned toward me. "I'm not telling you this because I want you to tell her for me. I'll do it. I'm just practicing. If I say it out loud to someone, then it'll be easier to say it out loud to her."

I nodded. "You're brave, Robert. You'll figure it out."

And like a wave, it hit me. Understanding washed over and tumbled me about as if I was a little girl on the shore. They'd been acting just like Daddy and Muriel. Of course he liked Honey, and I now realized that Honey liked him too. I'd noticed their interactions at times, just like I'd noticed Daddy and Muriel's.

"Margaret!" Robert pointed, his voice in panic. "Your room is on fire!"

I nearly fell off the roof. "Holy Jesus!"

I turned around but couldn't move. Black smoke poured into the night.

"The candles!"

I couldn't go back through my window, and no other

window opened onto the roof. I scooted further down the side of the house as hot smoke billowed out the front.

In an instant, Robert disappeared and was pounding on our door to wake Daddy. I yelled for Daddy too, hoping my frightened voice would get through his deep sleep and snoring. One of the neighbors came out then disappeared back into his house. I prayed he was calling the fire department.

In seconds, Daddy appeared below me, Robert at his side.

"Can you get me down?" I yelled.

Daddy squinted up at me as Robert ran to the garage for the ladder. When he returned, Daddy sprang toward it and helped Robert raise it to the second floor. Daddy footed the ladder as I climbed down. For once, I appreciated that he made me climb up on the roof every summer.

"Margaret," Daddy said, breathing hard and smoothing my hair, "you were so smart to go out on the roof. Are you okay?"

Robert and I exchanged a quick glance. "Yeah, I'm okay." I let him hug me while we watched the flames come out the window and distant sirens wail their way closer.

The firemen arrived in minutes and knocked down the flames. Water leaked from the hose connections and poured down the side of the house. It was a disaster, and it was all my fault.

I said nothing as we stood in our pajamas, enveloped by the muggy September night, trying to compose the competing excuse and apology in my head. Each time I was ready to tell Daddy the truth, he looked at me proudly and patted my arm, leaving me unable to shatter his opinion.

When the kindly fire captain came out of the house with something in his hand, my heart sank. "Mr. Thibodeaux, we found this candle and a few others in that upstairs bedroom. They might have been the source. We think the fire damage is confined to the bedroom, but we'll have to poke holes in the ceiling to make sure there's no fire in the attic. Water sure makes a mess, though."

Daddy nodded at the captain, then turned to me. I tried to look him in the eyes. I really did.

"Margaret, did you have lit candles in your room?"

I bit my lip. "Yes, sir."

"What happened?"

"Robert called me out onto the roof, and I forgot about them. I'm sorry."

Daddy looked at Robert like he was deciding if the reprimand should be directed his way too. "Did you know about the candles?"

Robert glanced at me, a definite "sorry" in his eyes. "No, sir," he said quietly.

He turned back to me. "What were you doing with the candles?"

"Relaxing."

It was true. Partly. The rest was best left unsaid.

Daddy's arms hung by his side. He bowed his head, and for a moment, I thought he was praying. Then he lifted his head and said to me in a whisper, "Why don't you walk over to Honey's house and stay with her tonight?" He made a sideways head gesture. "Goodnight, Robert." Then he turned and trudged up the front steps, stopping once to gently pat the porch pillar.

Lying in the twin bed next to Honey's that night, my heart heavy with guilt for almost destroying our house, and sadness that candles would never be part of my meditations again, a realization struck me and I bolted upright.

Mama's things!

Chapter 30

Wednesday, September 11, 1974

That next morning, after a restless night of worry, the sun was barely up when I sneaked out of Honey's room and out the front door. I ran all the way home and held my breath as I turned the handle.

Daddy was already sitting in the kitchen with a cup of coffee and a cigarette in his hand.

When I appeared in the doorway, the look in his eyes told me my worst fears were about to be spelled out in ash.

He sighed and flicked the cigarette with practiced steadiness. "Some of your stuff got burned and smoke-ruined."

I swallowed hard against a desert-dry mouth.

"I'm sorry, Pea . . . Mama's things got ruined too."

Tears welled instantly. I looked at the ceiling to keep them from spilling, but it didn't work. They poured down my face in twin rivers.

"What did you do with them?" I managed.

Daddy sighed again. He shaped the ember into a neat cone. "Her picture was seared . . . and the perfume bottle was broken."

I bit my lips together as the tears dripped from my jawline. "And the rest?" I whispered when I thought my voice wouldn't quiver.

"The rosary . . . it smells awful . . . and we'll never get the smell out of the pearls. The crucifix and glove were smoke-ruined too. I had to throw most of it away."

"What? You didn't have to throw anything away! I would have cleaned them!"

Daddy kept his tone soft and comforting. "Yes, I did, Pea. You can't get smoke out. You can't undo some things."

"I would have fixed them!"

"You have her ring . . . and we have more pictures. In the attic, I think."

I hadn't taken Mama's wedding ring off since I placed it on my pinky when I was grounded. I was relieved it had escaped the flames, but the rest . . .

I threw myself into the chair across from Daddy and buried my head in my arms. "It's all I had of her," I sobbed. "It's almost all I had!"

Daddy smoothed my hair the way he did when I was little, and I didn't pull away.

Later that morning, I moved into the downstairs guest bedroom. Daddy had brought down the clothes that survived in my closet and dresser, then closed off my room because of the smell and the repairs that needed to be done.

As calm as Daddy was right after the fire, he let me have it over the next few days with words that hit hard:

"Well, you've blown a hole in the roof of the garage and damned near burned the house down. What's next?"

"They should have named the hurricane Margaret. You did more damage than Carmen did."

And the worst one: "What would your mama think of what you've done this summer?"

I didn't fight back, knowing I was lucky we'd caught the fire before it destroyed our beautiful Farmhouse, which had been in Daddy's family for almost a hundred years. Strangely enough, I wasn't grounded. I didn't question it, and on Saturday morning, I went to the Talking Tree with Honey and Robert. The rock in my gut was still there, but since the fire didn't dislodge it, I now attributed it to the nerves of starting high school in only ten days.

We all three ran for the swings and soared as high as we could go, letting the stress of the past few days dissipate through laughter.

When we settled down to a normal swing, with Honey

and me in sync, I turned to her. "Hey . . . I found out about the poems."

"You did?"

"Yep. I had an argument with Daddy during the storm, and he told me *he* put them there . . . that he found them in old man Merriweather's trash, or they escaped from his trash . . . and he liked them . . . so he's been putting them there for years. You and I found the last two."

"Oh, Margaret. That's such a relief. But I didn't know you had an argument with your daddy."

"Yeah. It was pretty intense.

Robert chimed in. "Are you talking about your daddy putting something on your mama's grave?"

I turned to him. "How do you know he did that?"

"I saw him do it once or twice . . . when I was playing catch with a few guys from the team in that field near the cemetery. He walked up to the tree and laid something down on one of the graves."

My mouth dropped open. "So if we had told you we found poems on Mama's grave, you would have known it was Daddy?"

He tipped his head. "Yeah . . . I think—"

Robert stopped mid-sentence as brakes squealed behind us. A slight bend in the road prevented us from seeing the car, but there was no mistaking the screech of tires, followed by a thunderous splash. A strip of grass lay between the road and the bayou, but it was not enough to stop a speeding car from plunging into the hurricane-swollen water.

Robert jumped from the swing and took off running. Honey and I followed close behind as he dove into the water, the ripples of the crash flaying outward. The bayou was so murky that he immediately disappeared.

Honey and I rushed to the water's edge. The rain-softened ground gave beneath our shoes. Just a few feet away, black streaks of burned rubber left their mark on the street, and deep ruts cut through the grass to where the car entered the bayou.

Robert came up for air as the dark blue Mustang filled with water. He took a huge breath and submerged himself again. It seemed like forever, like it always does when something horrible is happening.

Finally, Robert appeared with David limp in his arms.

As Robert swam toward us, the back end of the car hesitated only moments before sinking below the surface.

Suddenly, David flailed, his body reacting to an insult his mind hadn't processed yet.

"Is anyone else in the car?" Robert yelled.

David's head lolled, and he choked up water. Robert heaved him onto the bank, not waiting for an answer. He turned and dove again toward the sunken car.

I heard sirens get louder and louder. "They're coming," I assured Honey.

She nodded but kept her eyes on the water. When Robert came up for a breath, she shouted, "Help's coming!" but he went under again, leaving a trail of bubbles.

Honey and I scanned the surface for Robert, abject fear

thrown between us. I didn't know Robert could hold his breath that long.

A police car screeched to a halt. Two officers jogged toward us.

"My friend is looking for two boys in the car, and he hasn't come up," Honey screamed. "Please save him!"

The words sent a chill through my soul as one cop tore off his gun belt and dove in. More rescuers arrived, some in their own cars. Three men dove into the bayou.

I could hear my breathing, loud as a church bell clanging in my chest, against Honey's incessant cries of "Hurry, hurry, hurry!"

The seconds stretched like hours until the men finally surfaced. Everyone faded into the background as my vision tunneled and I heard the words, "We couldn't get him loose. We need to raise the car."

I watched, detached, as the wrecker waded down into the water with the rescuers and dove to the bumper to affix the chain. Once back in the tow truck, he slowly pulled the car up. Water gushed from the open windows of David's beloved Mustang. The driver lowered the car onto the grass and the cop opened the back door.

Robert was in the backseat, his arm tangled in the seatbelt. Dead.

No one else was in the car.

CHAPTER 31

Tuesday, September 17, 1974

For three days before the funeral, I felt Robert around me. At random times, and when I wasn't paying attention to anything in particular, I heard pebbles against the window or the sound of a baseball hitting a glove. Once, when I was walking out my front door, I even heard him laugh. Oh, God, I heard him laugh. When I'd walk alone to the Talking Tree, I felt him leaning against it or sitting on the swings—the middle one, to be exact.

The rock in my gut was gone, but it had been replaced by the familiar and constant weight of grief. Robert felt different from Mama, though, maybe because I was more used to his presence in real life.

The funeral Mass both drew me and repelled me. I'd never had the sensation of yearning to be at church and at the same time felt sick to be there. Honey and I sat in the front row and held hands the entire time. It turned out to be a mistake, the front row. The casket was open, and Robert looked like he was merely sleeping in the white satin-lined box.

It was torture to sit and listen to platitudes about how things were and how things should be. Things were all fucked up, and nothing would ever be the same again. I wore my veil because I didn't want anyone to see my tears, but they all stared at me anyway, with pity, or sadness, or whatever it was people who didn't know the person who died felt. Honey wept throughout the service. My rosary lay untouched in my lap.

It surprised me that so many school friends were in attendance. Some of them ugly-cried the brutal sounds of grief, but the priest ignored the outbursts and didn't comfort any of us. We wanted to be seen. Our lovely friend was gone and we were distraught, but Father Archibald was having none of it.

That day, I found a new thing to be mad at the Church for.

The priest swung incense over the casket. It wafted up, like little spirits ascending to heaven, as if the scented smoke absolved the world for the sin of taking my friend. The pungent smell stung. I put a gloved hand over my mouth and nose as a barrier to the burning that neither cleansed nor purified what had happened.

When we rose for communion, the only part of Mass I recognized through tears, I walked toward my Savior without expectation, without hope. Inside, I railed against His will, stamping my foot like a child impatient with His demands.

In the quiet place still allowed for God to work miracles, I took the Body and comfort descended upon me, a calm as if someone had laid a shroud over me from head to foot. I returned to the pew and prayed on my knees. Ever so briefly, Robert sat to my left. I put my hand on the bench, but it was only wood.

"Tell her kindergarten yellow," I heard him say.

It didn't make any sense.

I knew then that he was really gone.

When the service concluded, the priest invited the congregation to pass by the casket, starting with those seated in the back and moving forward. Being in the front row meant we were trapped. We had no choice but to watch as, one by one, each person viewed Robert lying on display.

It had given me momentary comfort to see Robert when I arrived, but I didn't want to see this. The more I watched the congregants stare and cry and make their heartbreaking little gestures toward him, the more the hysteria rose in my throat, making me choke and struggle to breathe.

When our turn finally came, a wail rose from Honey.

I immediately had to get out of that high-ceilinged place reserved for reverence and quiet contemplation of His wonder, unable to bear watching as Honey and his mama said goodbye. I rushed down the nave and out the front door. The hundreds of people who had left the building before me were gathered in small groups of solace. As if responding to a conductor, they all looked up in unison, transfixed by my presence. Seconds ticked by with no sound. And then my voice, desperate and out of control, erupted from deep inside me and I fell into the arms of someone near.

It wasn't until Honey and Robert's mama emerged, bawling with the same heartbreak, did I realize it was Muriel who held me, and that the person beside her patting my arm was Daddy.

Muriel stood me upright, dried my tears with a pretty pink handkerchief, and put a dry one in my hand. Honey made her way to us and I noticed Jezebel in the distance. She waved to me through the crowd but didn't make a move to come talk to us. I waved back then reached for Honey's hand.

Neither Honey nor I could stand talking to anyone. It's one thing to chat with someone who has had the same experience as you, but when they can't relate because it's never happened to them, a chasm appears that is impossible to span with words. Just like when Mama died, the world should have stopped turning, but it just kept on.

When we got to my house, Honey said she'd rather go home and lie down, that she didn't feel so good.

I let her go and tried to find something to distract me, but the house wasn't comforting. I couldn't go upstairs, and the guest room where I was sleeping didn't feel familiar, so I went for a walk.

Jezebel opened her door before I even knocked. She stepped onto the porch with a hug as a greeting, then led me inside. All the curtains were open, making the room light and bright in contrast to Jezebel, who looked worn and weepy.

I went straight to the kitchen to make us some tea. I felt

the need to delay talk of Robert, so I spent time loading the serving tray, then rummaged in the pantry for some cookies. I even steeped both our tea bags until the hot water turned amber.

When I returned to the living room, Jezebel was in her rocker, staring into space. I set the tray on the coffee table and served her tea with a saucer underneath, a cookie beside the dainty white cup with red roses and gold rim.

She thanked me and I sat across from her. "I can't stop seeing him running and diving and not coming up."

Jezebel said nothing, just smiled at me like she was trying to warm up the room.

Now I was the one who hated silence.

Finally, she said, "Try to 'tink of his laugh. 'Dat's what he'd want from us."

I sighed. "I can't imagine ever laughing again. He made me laugh for the first time after Mama died. He put mud pies in his freezer next to the hamburger. His mama was so mad when they thawed out."

Jezebel let out a light chuckle. "If anyone can make you laugh 'tru sadness, it's Robert."

"I've felt him a few times. Do you think I always will? Like Mama?"

"Maybe yes, maybe no. You need to feel him to know he's around us? 'Dat he's wit' us always?"

I'd never thought of it that way. Maybe they were always around, like they were just sitting in the next room. I shouldn't need to see them or hear them or feel them to know they were here. But the knowing was hard. Belief, yes, but knowing was deeper, and I wasn't there yet.

On my way home, I stopped by Honey's house to check on her. She was lying on the couch with a blanket, even though it was seventy-eight degrees outside. Honey's house was cold like mine and Jezebel's; the grown-ups spent good money on central air, and they used it.

I knelt down next to her. "How are you doing?"

"He saved my asshole brother." It was the first time I'd ever heard Honey swear. Maybe it didn't count because her voice was so flat. "I wish he'd let him die. I'd rather have Robert than David any day."

I was not prepared for this from her. "It was brave, what he did," I offered.

"It was stupid."

Honey seemed far away, and I didn't like it. But I didn't try to talk her out of being angry because I agreed with her in principle; I just couldn't summon the energy to feel it.

"Want to go for a walk?" I asked, anxious for movement.

She hesitated, then said, "Sure."

As we walked down the middle of Legard Street, it was like sucking on a milkshake, pulling in the thick, humid air every time we took a breath. We didn't want to think about what had happened; we didn't want to talk about it either. But at the moment, it was the only thing that seemed to exist in our world and next to impossible to get away from.

The crickets sang loudly from the bayou, accompanied by the hum of thousands of bugs.

"Margaret," Honey ventured, "did he ever, you know, talk about me?"

Honey looked pained, and I couldn't decide if she just wondered or if she missed him and wanted to talk about him like I talked about Mama.

"Yeah," I said. "He talked about you the night of the fire. I didn't know before then."

"What did he say?"

"He said you weren't the kind of girl he wanted to date."

Honey huffed. "Well, that's not very nice."

I stopped walking and turned to her, clasping her arm. "He said you were the kind of girl he wanted to marry."

Honey stood still for a few seconds, then her shoulders gave way to her sobs.

Chapter 32

Thursday, September 26, 1974

The grown-ups had forced us to start school on Monday, but we hated every minute of it—even Honey, which was akin to the end of the world.

The rain came down hard. Honey arrived on my porch with her coat and dress soaked. She had called out sick the day before, so I hadn't expected her to show up today. When she greeted me, she sounded tired. But what made alarm creep up my throat were her pale lips and sunken eyes. She looked like an old lady and not a young girl.

"I'm sick," she said.

"What's wrong? Did your mother take you to the doctor?" I motioned her into the house, but she shook her head.

"I haven't told Mother, and she hasn't noticed. I wanted to ask you first..."

"Ask me?"

"... if I could talk to Miss Muriel, you know, without worrying my folks."

A tightness gripped my jaw thinking of how I'd responded to Honey's worship of Muriel. Honey might have gone to her sooner if I hadn't been so vocal about loyalty, and so obstinate about not letting Muriel into my family. Honey was sicker than she needed to be because of me.

"Let's go talk to her right now," I said. "Can you ride your bike?"

"I think so . . . but we'll have to go slow. The rain, you know." Honey didn't like excuses, so when she made one, dread set its claws into my chest.

I put on my raincoat and ran around to the garage to get my bike, then we rode through the rain to Muriel's office. As we entered, a little bell announced two drenched girls with brown streaks up their backs. Dirty water had sprayed from the bike's back tires, and my hair had road grime mixed in. I smoothed it down and wiped my hand on my plaid skirt, then approached the receptionist.

"I'm Margaret. Jimmy's Margaret. May we see Dr. Lafleur, please?"

"Doctor is with a patient right now." She looked Honey and me up and down. "Can you wait . . . um . . . on the porch?" She pointed to a pair of white wicker chairs outside. "I'll let you know when she's done."

I didn't take offense at being asked to go outside like a dog. Yesterday I would have, but today, Honey was what mattered.

We sat staring out at the street, watching ladies wearing

bell-bottom jeans swish past on their way to shop downtown.

I swiveled to face Honey. "When did this start?"

She sighed. "I thought I was just really sad about Robert but . . . I didn't feel very good before . . . before he died." She held my hand. "I'm scared."

"You'll be okay," I encouraged. "I noticed you were acting different, but I didn't realize you were sick. I'm sorry if you tried to tell me and I didn't listen."

"It's not your fault . . . I tried hard not show it. I thought it would just go away . . . but then, over the last week, it got worse."

No matter my feelings about Muriel, Honey needed my support. I wasn't about to make her more afraid than she already was. I squeezed her hand. "Miss Muriel will have you fixed up in no time. She's an excellent doctor."

Honey nodded. We waited in silence until the receptionist called us in and ushered us into Muriel's office. As Honey sat ladylike in a chair, my defiance of the last few months softened. I needed something from Muriel, and I needed to trust her too, for Honey. I'd thought it was grief making Honey so listless, but if I was being honest with myself, I'd noticed it before the accident. I needed to be honest with myself from now on.

Muriel entered with a smile. "This is a surprise. What can I do for you, ladies?" I marveled she was even civil to me. Her face changed to concern when she looked at Honey.

"I'm sick," Honey said.

Muriel pulled a chair up to Honey and took her hands. "Have you told your mother?"

Honey stared into her lap. "No, ma'am. I thought I was just sad, so I didn't want to bother anyone. But now I feel worse, and I don't think it's just sadness. I wondered if you could tell me if it's physical or really bad grief."

My heartbeat sped up as real and honest fear invaded my body, not some fear I'd made up in my head.

"Describe how you feel," said Muriel.

"I'm tired. And I'm thirsty all the time. I'm dizzy. Now I'm nauseated too. Maybe I'm just sad about . . . you know."

Muriel turned Honey's hands over and back, felt her pulse, and asked her to open her mouth and say ahhh. Muriel started to speak but then closed her mouth without saying anything.

"What is it?" Honey's voice cracked.

Muriel leaned in closer. "Oh, Honey, I didn't mean to scare you. My hesitation is that your folks don't know you're here and I'm not a pediatrician. You need to have your mother take you to the hospital. Tell her I said you should go. The fatigue and dizziness can be from grief, but the thirst and nausea has me concerned."

Honey turned to me, then back to Muriel.

Muriel squeezed her arm gently. "Let's call your mother and I'll explain to her that you need to go to the ER now. All the symptoms you describe can be diabetes. Finding out if you have it is as simple as a few tests, but you should go today. I can't tell if you have it or how bad, so please, go today.

You could die if it's diabetes and you don't have it treated."

Honey sat ramrod straight, taking the news in her stoic way, but those simple words shot through my heart like lead going three thousand feet per second. I imagined Honey dying. I could see it, feel it. It would probably kill me too.

CHAPTER 33

Monday, September 30, 1974

Honey spent the next few days at St. Joseph's Hospital undergoing tests and treatments. I knew what type 1 diabetes was in general, but learning more would be helpful and not make things harder than they already were for Honey. Most of all, I wanted her home. Hospitals were not my favorite place.

At supper on Sunday, I asked Muriel why Honey got sick.

Muriel paused. "It's complicated, and sometimes we don't know for sure. But her pancreas isn't making insulin anymore."

"Is it permanent?" I asked.

"Unfortunately, yes. She'll have it her whole life."

"What about Halloween? Can she still eat candy?"

Daddy sat back and grinned at our exchange as Muriel laughed. "That depends on how she controls her sugar. She has to inject insulin based on what her sugar is, but then she has to eat, so it makes it hard to regulate at first."

I took a bite of the chocolate cake Muriel had baked for dessert. "I hope I don't get diabetes."

In true Honey fashion, she took to the new routine of daily testing and logging her meals with ease. I never heard her complain to the doctors, nurses, or her mother; the only thing she said about it was, "This whole testing thing is inefficient."

"How so?" I asked her.

"Stick yourself with a needle, get a result, do it again a few hours later, continue for life. Seems like there could be a way to always know what your sugar is, like the heart monitor."

I was thrilled to hear analytical Honey, but her voice held a sadness that I feared would be there forever.

On Friday, Daddy let me call in sick from school so that I could ride with Mrs. Sinclair to pick up Honey from the hospital. Though she was upright and dressed in her clothes, she'd lost weight, and she still looked sick. She was better, but not the Honey I was used to.

I looked her straight in the eye so she knew I wasn't just asking a polite question. "How do you feel?"

Honey sighed. "Tired. I'm so tired." It didn't come out like a complaint. It was a fact.

Honey moved in slow motion as we settled her into the car, giving me a glimpse of what she would be like as an old woman. I watched her closely from the back seat the whole way home. She broke my heart when she reached up to touch the window glass as we passed Robert's house.

Muriel was at Honey's when we pulled up in the drive. She was the perfect distraction to keep Mrs. Sinclair from hovering. Honey's mother had been ever-present in the hospital, and Honey rolled her eyes when she fussed. After not noticing for weeks that her daughter had a major medical problem, she was going to make up for it now by giving Honey the utmost attention.

Lucky for us, we got permission to go to Honey's room by ourselves to get her settled back in. Honey placed her testing kit on the dresser, not bothering to ask her mother if it was okay, while I unpacked her small suitcase. Afterward, we both lay on her twin beds, staring up at the ceiling. This time, it was my turn to keep Honey's mind from drifting to things she couldn't change.

"The Baldwin twins cut their hair," I said. "I mean *cut* it. They look like boys now."

No response.

"What do you think of the boys who wear their hair long?" I grabbed the decorative pillow behind me and held it to my chest. "I don't like it. Makes them look messy. Crew cuts for me. I was born in the wrong decade."

"Hmm," Honey said.

I turned to her and her eyes were closed. I got up and covered her with the throw blanket at the end of her bed, then slipped downstairs to sit with the grown-ups.

"Is she sleeping?" Mrs. Sinclair asked.

"Yeah, she fell asleep after I put her stuff away."

"Thank you for helping."

I hadn't meant to garner thanks. "Of course. Anything for Honey."

Muriel offered me coffee, and I neglected to tell her I'd never had it before. After taking a bitter sip of blackness, I set the cup down and reached for the cream and sugar. Four teaspoons and a long pour later, I enjoyed my first cup of coffee.

Mrs. Sinclair turned to me. "She's going to be home from school for a week or so. Would you bring her homework to her?"

"Oh," I said, disappointed. "I didn't know she wouldn't be going right back. But that makes sense. Hard to concentrate when you're tired and your sugar is all over the place." I glanced at Muriel to gauge if my guess was right and she nodded with a smile. "Will it take her long to get the right dose? So she can come back to school?"

Mrs. Sinclair spun toward Muriel.

"Like we discussed," Muriel said kindly, "it depends. But with Honey, as smart as she is, not long."

That same warm kinship I first felt at Muriel's house surfaced again, and this time I allowed it to blanket me.

Chapter 34

Saturday, October 5, 1974

I decided to head over to Honey's for a visit and found Muriel's car in the drive. I hesitated, then decided I would take this opportunity to be nice to her for all the help she'd been with Honey.

Mrs. Sinclair and Muriel were sitting in the kitchen. Muriel held a coffee mug with both hands, and her engagement ring caught the morning sunlight streaming in through the window.

"Good morning," I said to them both. "Your ring sparkles in the sun," I said to Muriel with a smile on top.

"Honey might not be awake yet," Mrs. Sinclair cautioned.

"I'll be quiet and let her sleep if she's not," I assured her.

I climbed the stairs and slipped into her room. Honey was still in her pajamas, sleeping, so I sat in the chair near the foot of her bed and stared at her. Honey's skin was pale, and she seemed to be breathing funny. I jumped up and ran back to the kitchen.

"Something's wrong with Honey," I said.

Muriel rushed to Honey's room while I stood frozen on the spot. There was nothing I could do but trust Muriel to save Honey—and to save me. Honey said long ago that we would be friends our whole lives. I thought our lives would be longer.

I bolted out of the house and down the street toward the Talking Tree. As I neared our beloved space, the image of Robert running toward the bayou, full speed to his end, played like a movie. Our tree was no longer a respite either.

The dappled shadows from the trees flashed me back to that day long ago when I'd stood at the window, waiting for mourners to arrive. I remembered thinking the trees didn't have the sense to know it was a terrible day. Sometimes, I hadn't had any more sense than a tree myself.

I wandered a few blocks this way and a few that way, eventually passing the elementary school. The swings swayed back and forth, as if an unseen child just left them to run off and play somewhere else. On the strip of grass between the sidewalk and the street, a child's glove lay forgotten on the blanket of green. I picked it up and patted the soft cotton, which was surprisingly white for having been thrown away or lost. The fallen leaves caught the wind and swirled around me as I held the glove to my cheek. I looked to see if anyone nearby had dropped it, but no one was around, so I slid it into my back pocket.

I hadn't intended it, but I arrived at the cemetery, pulled like a bird going north for the winter. I opened the gate and willed myself through it.

Robert's new casement was to the left of the entry. I stopped and crossed myself at his feet.

"Eternal rest grant unto him, O Lord, and let perpetual light shine upon him. May he rest in peace. Amen."

I felt him next to me, always on my left.

"Hi, Robert."

Concrete's not my thing. I prefer grass.

I wasn't sure he said it, but it was something he would say, and I smiled.

After a few tearful minutes, Mama's grave tugged at my middle. I said goodbye to Robert, crossed myself again, then made my way across the expanse of green grass. Two yellow roses and a pink envelope lay on the grave. I'd never seen flowers in the holder or on the marker before, only the ones Honey and I brought. I opened the flap and pulled the notecard from inside.

In a fluid script was written: *I'll take care of them both, I promise.*

I bent my head, tears spilling down my face. I replaced the note in the envelope and set it near Mama's name, then took the white glove from my pocket and placed it on Mama's grave. It seemed like it should be there too.

I wiped my face with my palm, and a mist like the evening fog appeared on my cheeks. I sensed a presence to my right and turned toward it. It was Mama, real and vibrant, wearing a pink dress.

"Mama?" I said aloud.

It flashed through my mind that it wasn't Mama, that it

was an evil spirit like Honey said. But Honey was wrong.

Mama nodded and spoke to me, not out loud, but the words were as clear as any conversation I'd ever had.

It was an accident.

My heart leapt at confirmation of what I'd known all along.

"Are you in heaven?"

I'm everywhere.

I stood mesmerized, thinking about Mama and Daddy and Muriel.

"I don't know about Muriel." It was a declarative sentence, not a question.

I sent her.

"You sent who?"

Muriel.

"Mother of God, Mama. Why?"

This time, the answer didn't come in actual words. Instead, a sense of protection, comfort, and love descended on me. It was like Mama wrapping me from head to toe in her whole body, ethereal as it was.

"But why? Why her?"

Muriel is an angel.

I couldn't help being pertinacious. "Literal or figurative?"

But Mama didn't answer. She began singing the lullaby then drifted away, like Daddy's mind did when I asked too many questions. I reached out to keep her, but she was nothing but mist.

Mama had sent Muriel.

I'd expected the answer to be, "Your daddy deserves to be happy; he has my blessing." Or, "You can accept Muriel as your new mother." Or even, "Keep fighting; she's not who she seems." But never this. Never "I sent her."

"Can my mind really change, just like snapping my fingers?" I said. I probably sounded like a crazy person speaking out loud, in a cemetery of all places, but I'd never felt less crazy in my life. I turned my hands over and back as if inspecting them would give me a clue about what had just happened. There was no denying it. Like a strategic chess move, Muriel had moved to a position of strength, representing the Muriel Honey saw, not the one I had seen all these months.

I ran once again, but this time, I blazed home to Daddy.

Breathless by the time I burst through the back door, I stopped just inside.

Daddy was sitting at the breakfast table. "Oh, thank God," he said, appearing relieved to see me. "Muriel called and said you ran off. Honey's okay. Muriel was worried about you."

I brought my hand to my heart. "I was scared to death that Honey was dying, and I had to get away. I couldn't stand it if she abandoned me too."

"Abandoned?"

"Deserted, cast off. Left without my permission. Mama abandoned me. Robert abandoned me. I couldn't stand it if Honey did."

Daddy motioned me toward him. "Aw, Pea. Folks dying—they aren't abandoning you. They aren't doing it to you on purpose."

"That's what I ran home to tell you." I sat in my spot across from him. "I figured it out."

Daddy sat forward and snuffed out his cigarette.

"I'm afraid of it, of being abandoned . . . like you said during the storm. But Mama—she said she's everywhere. She's not gone. Maybe I was afraid if I let Muriel in, she'd leave too."

"That's a pretty grown-up conclusion. What do you mean she said she's everywhere?"

"I went to the cemetery to talk to Mama like I've been trying to do for months." Daddy sighed, but I hurried on. "But on the way, I knew I had to trust Muriel to save Honey. So, if I could trust her with that . . . I should be able to trust her to stay if . . . if I accepted her."

Daddy leaned back, a smile widening his face.

"And then I found a note she wrote to Mama . . . it was on her grave . . . it's really sweet. And then I saw Mama."

Daddy raised a brow. "You saw her? Actually saw her?"

"Yes, Daddy. She said it was an accident, her dying, and she sent Muriel, and she's everywhere. I like the everywhere part. And if Mama sent Muriel to you, to us, well then . . . I have to be more welcoming."

Daddy narrowed his eyes. My jaw ached with tension and a sudden fear that he'd call bullshit on this too. Instead, he made a "hm" sound and got up to refill his coffee. He pulled the cream from the ice box and brought a cup to me too. The sugar bowl already graced the table.

He sat back down. "What was she wearing?"

"A pink dress." I stirred in the cream and added four sugars. "Long sleeves, with a boat neckline."

Daddy rubbed his eyebrow, as if to rub out a stubborn stain of memory. "That's the one I buried her in. I bought it new, just for. . . . You never saw it."

"I know."

"Then how?"

"I told you, Daddy, I can feel and hear her. And then today, I saw her too. That's why I don't act like she's gone."

Daddy's gaze lingered on me as he took a long sip of his coffee, as if he both questioned my sanity and believed me all at once.

I returned to Honey's house to find her sitting up in bed, knees drawn up, drinking some broth. Muriel was gone, and Mrs. Sinclair was hovering.

"What happened?" I asked.

"Where did you go?"

"I had to leave. I . . . thought you were dying."

"Well, technically, I was. But Miss Muriel gave me some sugar, and that fixed it. I guess I still don't have the insulin dose right."

"Is this going to be a regular occurrence?"

"Not if I can help it." Honey smiled, and the life force that was Honey Sinclair shone through. Relief was an understatement.

"Mother, thank you, I don't need anything else right now."

Mrs. Sinclair took the hint with a polite smile, then closed the door behind her.

I sat on the foot of Honey's bed. "Can the way you see something change in an instant?"

Honey set her broth on the nightstand. "Well . . . getting a diagnosis like diabetes definitely changes things right away. And Robert . . ." She lowered her voice. "All of it's more than changed how I see everything."

I was such an ass. I was asking her opinion about something in *my* head, not the world-crushing things she was going through. I opened my mouth, but nothing came out.

Graciously, she asked, "What do you mean? Is there something you suddenly see differently?"

I ran my hand over her white coverlet with its little tufts of flowers. "Oh, Honey, I'm sorry. I'm so selfish sometimes. I'll be better, I promise."

"It's okay. You're allowed to be selfish when we're young. Just don't stay that way, okay?"

The words stung but I nodded.

She straightened herself against the pillows. "What's changed how you see something in an instant?"

I took in a breath. "I talked to Mama."

"Oh geez, not that again." Honey bent her head to her knees.

"No, Honey, I actually *talked* to her. I saw her at the cemetery."

"You what?" Honey looked up, wide-eyed.

"She said her dying was an accident and that she sent Miss Muriel . . . that she was an angel, just like you've said all those times."

Honey opened her mouth, but before she could say anything, I added, "So I'm okay with it now. No more pushing against her or Daddy . . . or you."

Honey slowly relaxed against the pillows. "Are you sure it was her? Did you maybe just want to see her so bad that you imagined it?" Her question was probing, but not dismissive.

"I thought that for a second—what if it's *not* Mama, like you say. But it was her."

"Did you see Robert?"

"No . . . but I felt him."

Honey took a deep breath. "Yes, I think when you have an experience like that, everything can change." She paused, then asked, "Do you feel Robert the way you feel your mama?"

I nodded. "I do."

Honey leaned toward me. "I heard him laugh."

"What? You did? When?"

"When we got home from the hospital. I was talking to Mother, and we were looking at picture albums. You know how she's helping with Robert's dad's case."

I nodded again.

"Well, she was the one who went to Angola to tell him Robert died. Then I got sick. It's been a bit much for her. Anyway, I pointed to a picture of myself on my first day of kindergarten, and I heard him laugh.

"Kindergarten yellow," I whispered.

Honey's mouth dropped open. "I was wearing a yellow dress. How did you know?"

"Robert told me at the funeral. He said, 'Tell her kindergarten yellow,' but it didn't make any sense then. He told me so you would know it was him. He was there. He's everywhere."

Honey closed her eyes. A smile played on her face that told me maybe, just maybe, she was starting to believe it too.

Chapter 35

Sunday, October 6, 1974

The next day, after sleeping until 11:00 a.m., I got up and dressed, then walked to Jezebel's for answers and comfort, in that order.

Jezebel did not seem surprised to see me, nor did she say much. She had a tray already set. I poured us tea, and we took our usual places in the living room.

Honey's question about the cemetery encounter had dug its way into my confidence. "Did I just imagine seeing Mama because I wanted it so much?" I asked her.

"Did you do 'de 'tings I said to tell 'de difference? Try to change some'ting?"

I bit the inside of my cheek. "No, I didn't think of it. I just knew it was her."

"Well, 'den, I'm sure it was her."

"But that's never happened before. I've never seen her.

I've only felt and heard her." My new hesitation to accept what I'd seen with my own eyes was the last defense. Against what, I wasn't sure.

"You upset?"

"Of course I am." I wiggled on the couch, agitated.

"So, if spirits want to get 'tru to you, 'dey need to give you proof first?"

I shrugged.

"Tell me, when you meet your friend on 'de street, you ask 'dem for proof of who 'dey are?"

"No . . . because I know them."

"How you know 'dem?"

"I recognize them."

"And how you do 'dat?"

"I don't know," I said, frustrated by a line of questioning I didn't understand.

"Let me ask you 'dis. You trust yourself? What you feel, what you know?"

I nodded. "Yes. Most times."

"'Den, why you don't trust some'ting you experience, like seeing your mama?"

"I trust it. It just seems so unreal. So implausible."

"According to who?"

"Everyone, up until yesterday."

"Everyone?" She raised one eyebrow.

"Not you. You know what I mean. Until yesterday, everyone fought me. 'It can't be real. It's the devil,' they'd say. *I knew it was real, but when only one person thinks something* is real, they might be the crazy one. I didn't want to be the crazy one, and *that* was making me crazy."

Jezebel leaned back. "So, you got what you wanted?"

"Talking to Mama? Yes."

"'Den, why 'de fluster? Why you trying to disprove it to yourself now?"

"Because I got an answer that feels one hundred percent true. She'll always be around, but it contradicted everything I feared. Won't Miss Muriel think I'm lying if I'm suddenly on her side?" I turned my attention to pushing at a cuticle with my nail. "I need to apologize for the way I've treated her . . . and that's not my most curated skill."

Jezebel paused, then said, "Is your problem 'dat you don't trust yourself, or you afraid to trust o'ders?"

I popped my head up. "Wait—we're talking about trust?"

"You just told me you been wrong. Makes it hard to trust yourself. You trust Miss Muriel to still be around after you tell her what you did and apologize? Simple question."

"Oh." I hesitated. "I'm not sure there's a simple answer."

"Give it a try."

I looked down and continued smoothing the cuticle back and forth. "I'm sure of what I feel and see. But then, to me, Miss Muriel was conniving, even though the whole town loves her." I looked up at Jezebel.

"And . . ." she said.

"And I guess I realize now that she's who the town thought she was . . . and that I was wrong about her."

"Okay," she said, with a lilt that invited more from me.

"I thought talking to Mama would fix everything. It hasn't."

"Ahh. Trust is a skill, not a gift you give to someone."

"How so?"

Jezebel laid her hands on the arms of the chair and sat forward.

"You been learning it your whole life. When you a baby, you learn o'ders will care for you. You learn trust. It's not like an object you give to someone else. You learn, for every person you meet, how you trust 'dem. When you walk, you learn 'dat if you don't move your feet right, you fall down. You learn to trust your body. As you grow, you learn when your ideas are right and wrong. You learn to trust your mind. If trust is some'ting you learn, it's a skill 'dat can be learned over and over again, sometimes even wit' 'de same person or situation. You ever heard 'de expression 'get back on 'de horse'? It's not just about determination; it's about learning trust again after it all goes bad."

Jezebel paused and studied my face. I met her eyes and didn't look away.

"So, it's my choice to trust myself. My choice to trust Miss Muriel, that she'll stay."

"Yes. 'Dat's it. You decide if you learn 'de skill. It doesn't just happen to you. Once you know it's a skill, you have more control. It's not so mercurial."

"Mercurial? That's a new one."

"Yes. Like mercury. Elusive. Runs away from you."

"Oh, excellent. I like words."

"Me too, baby."

I smiled and gulped the last of my tea.

"Good insight from you, Miss Margaret." Jezebel sat back again. "You'll figure it out. It's like 'de chicken I asked you to get and bring to me. Doesn't matter how you do it; it matters 'dat you do it."

Jezebel's face was creased with weariness, a map of griefs old and new. I got up and patted the back of her hand, then kissed her on the cheek. "Thank you, Miss Jezebel."

Chapter 36

Monday, October 14, 1974

We had a half day at school, so I decided it was time to go see Muriel. I'd hoped I would run into her at our house or at Honey's, but I hadn't seen her for more than a week, missing her by minutes or hours. I couldn't involve Daddy. I needed the Muriel Acceptance to be just between us.

Cocooned in the balmy eighty-degree heat, wondering if butterflies felt the same sense of smothering before they emerged, I walked the mile to Muriel's office. When I arrived, I was scattered like a puzzle and wanted to at least have my borders arranged, so I stopped a moment to collect myself before opening the door.

"Is Dr. Lafleur available for lunch?" I asked Mrs. MacDonald, the receptionist.

She slid her glasses downward on her nose and scanned the appointment book. "I believe she is. Would you like me to pencil you in?"

"Yes, ma'am. What time does she break for lunch?"

"In about an hour. Come back, and I'll have sandwiches delivered for you from down the street."

She smiled at me and my stomach fluttered as I said "Thank you."

The bell tinkled as I stepped out, signaling the hour's start.

Time. It was exactly one month since Robert died, and I realized I was marking life against that event now instead of Mama's death.

As I wandered around, I passed the dress shop The Abomination had come from. I hurried past it, trying to distract myself, growing more nervous by the minute. I'd practiced my apology in the mirror, but I had no idea how Muriel would react to it.

After strolling into other shops to kill time, not remembering a thing I saw in any of them, it was finally almost noon. At five minutes till, the tinkling bell announced my return to the office. Mrs. MacDonald eyed me over her glasses and motioned for me to sit in one of the office chairs. At least I'd graduated to sitting inside.

Noon came and went. I picked up a magazine and flipped through it, not to look at any of the contents, but to make noise so Mrs. MacDonald would remember I was there. A few minutes later, the front door opened and a young boy entered, carrying a brown paper bag with the imprint of "Murphy's" on the side.

Muriel opened her office door as if she magically knew lunch had been delivered and motioned for me to come in. It took only seconds to cross the shrinking waiting room to her office—and to officially be on stage.

"Such a surprise to see you, Margaret," Muriel piped. "Mrs. MacDonald told me you wanted to have lunch."

She hadn't asked a question, so I wasn't sure how to open the conversation. I'd practiced what I was going to say and prayed it would come out as I intended.

I swallowed hard. "I'm sorry."

Muriel stopped mid-reach into the bag for the sandwiches. "Why are you sorry?"

"I'm sorry for the way I've acted toward you. I haven't been very nice."

She pulled the sandwiches out, handing one to me and placing the other in front of her. Sitting down, she said, "I hadn't noticed."

I swallowed again. Muriel wasn't making this easy. I was going to have to spell it out, confess and be absolved one sin by one.

"I've been ugly. I've been trying to make you go away, but you don't deserve to be treated like that, and I'm sorry. I'll change, I promise." My chin wobbled, but I got it under control.

Muriel came around the giant mahogany desk and motioned for me to sit. She brought the other patient chair close to me and sat down herself. "Look at me," she said kindly.

I looked up.

"I would have saved your mama if I could."

Tears.

"I'm sorry you lost her. I'm sorry your daddy lost her. But

we can't change it. The only thing we can do, and I hope we can do it together, is build a new family. It's like repairing a house after a storm."

I wiped my face. "So you're like the boards, and the hard work, and the coat of paint."

Muriel seemed surprised I'd picked up the analogy so quickly. "Yes, exactly."

I forced a smile.

Muriel lowered her voice. "Your daddy said your Mama's things you had in your room are ruined. Shall we honor her somewhere else in the house?"

That instant, the warm kinship returned, never to be pushed down again. I hadn't expected this, and I wasn't prepared with a ready answer. I thought for a moment. "What about yellow roses from our garden on the sideboard sometimes, in her vase?"

"That sounds lovely," she said, patting my hand. "I'll make sure we do that."

A giddy rush ran up my back. After all this time, it was such a simple resolution. Without having to detail every snide thing I'd done or said about her, she forgave me in an instant. And in that same instant, all the things Muriel had done, I appreciated.

As if reading my mind, she said, "Acceptance is hard, Margaret. I accept your apology, and I'm glad you've decided to accept me. Your daddy will be thrilled." She paused for a moment. "You know what's harder than changing?"

I shook my head.

"Letting someone else change. And I promise I'll let you."

It was a universal truth—that everyone changes—but I'd been doing exactly this, not letting others change, or at least not accepting it. Not Daddy, not Honey, not Muriel, not me. I needed to let change happen to all of us and quit fighting it. Change was as natural as rain on a Wednesday.

"Deal?" she asked playfully.

I nodded. "Deal."

We talked about the storm as we ate. Muriel told me about being in the hospital overnight with the power going out, but how every patient was attended to, most of them calm and trusting. I thanked her for saving Honey.

"I only did my job of taking care of people. I'm glad she's better."

"I couldn't stand it if she died too. I think you were meant to save her."

Muriel sighed gently with a smile. "We end up in the places we need to be, don't we?"

When I left Muriel's office, my stomach was no longer doing flip-flops, and I skipped down the steps.

As I headed home, David Sinclair stepped in front of me from the street. I jumped, not expecting anyone to impede my walk—David least of all.

"What do you want?" My words were curt, dismissive. I didn't find him at all cute anymore.

"To apologize."

"What for?" I knew what for, but he needed to say it.

When Robert died, the tightness of grief had been immediate. It was the most concrete sensation from Mama's death, and I was surprised it felt the same in my body with Robert. The memories, the sadness, they were different, but my body knew grief: a suffocating, immovable pressure in my chest. I stretched, walked, cried to make it go away, but nothing worked. I went numb from the magnitude of it, and I left the litter of my grief lying around for anyone to see. It had persisted in all its strength these last weeks until little by little, I didn't notice it as much. It had made me physically squirm, trying to shake it loose, to replace it with joy or some semblance of happiness. I got angry when someone laughed. How could anyone ever be happy again when Robert was gone? When the anger subsided, people's oblivious expressions offended me. Some days, I was still angry, especially at David.

He stood with his hands in his pockets and turned away from me. My eyes drilled into his face like a laser, willing him to meet my gaze. When he didn't, the words tumbled out.

"You can't just apologize. You have to change who and what you are. You have to show people time and time again that you're not reckless and dangerous. It's much harder to show people what you aren't than what you are. Everyone, *everyone*, is going to assume you'll continue being the self-involved asshole you've always been. You're going to have to be different for a long time before anyone will start seeing you differently."

David met my eyes and didn't flinch like I expected him to. He took the criticism and made no excuse. It was a start.

I stepped off the sidewalk into the street and crossed against the light. I wasn't sure where my words had come from. I'd meant them, but the tirade was not my style. As I walked, I turned the idea I'd spouted at David over in my head and realized it applied to me as well. Muriel might have accepted my apology, but it was a stretch to think the act signified some magical change, that it was instant evaporation of all I had done. I had work to do, not just learning trust like Jezebel suggested, but showing others I respected and valued them.

I changed course and headed to the cleaners. The Abomination was there for pressing when my room caught fire, so it escaped damage. If I was going to respect people and things, I might as well start with the dress.

Chapter 37

Saturday, October 19, 1974

Honey knocked on my door at 9:00 a.m. I greeted her and we stretched out on the front porch steps in the warm autumn sun. It was lovely in Louisiana this time of year, and it was the first Saturday in ages that we had nothing to do.

"Do you want to go to the Talking Tree?" Honey asked.

I shook my head. "I tried going there the day I ran off when you were sick. But . . . I knew when I got there that I couldn't be there anymore. It reminds me Robert isn't here, and I keep seeing him running toward the bayou. I'm not sure I'll ever go there again."

Honey was quiet as she absorbed my rationale. "Those swings will never be the same," she said in a soft and reverent voice.

"We'll find something."

"Yeah," she said, sullen at our losses. Then she turned to me. "Can we go to the cemetery? I want to put a cross on Robert's grave. It looks so . . . sad."

"Do you have one?"

"Actually, no. I didn't think that far."

An idea popped into my head. "Come on." I grabbed Honey's hand and ran around the house to the garage. The single bare bulb still cast the perfect amount of light.

"Daddy's got scrap wood, and we can cut it with the miter saw and then put nails in it to make a cross."

Honey surveyed the scraps of wood. "None of these look very nice. I want it to look nice."

"Okay, well . . . first we should ask Mrs. Pennington. For permission."

"I'll go ask her and you find the best pieces. Can we paint them white?"

"Sure. Daddy's got to have white paint. Everything in this house is white."

Honey skipped next door. It had been so quiet there these past weeks. When she returned, she was walking slowly, picking the petals off a daisy from Robert's front yard. "He loves me," she announced.

It was the little things she said that sometimes pained my heart. "Did she say it was okay?"

Honey nodded. "She just looks so sad."

"Maybe this will make her a little bit happy."

"I hope so."

By late afternoon, when the sun hung just under the tree

branches but didn't blind us, we finished Robert's cross and took it to Mrs. Pennington for final approval. She answered the door and nodded, her eyes filling with tears.

The cross was bigger than we'd intended. We had tried to make as few cuts as possible to create our monument, and we didn't have the patience or the time for refining and sanding. Three coats of paint would help it get through the six months until Robert's permanent stone arrived.

I hefted it over my shoulder for the walk to the cemetery, worried that I resembled Jesus on the path to Golgotha. It was only a few blocks, but still.

Honey led the way through the gates, and Robert's fresh gray casing, painfully centered in our vision, greeted us.

"How are we going to set it?" asked Honey. "We didn't bring anything to do it with."

"The gravel won't hold it either. Let's just rest it on the casement."

We set the cross at Robert's head and laid the end down at his feet. It tilted a little to my side and Honey righted it, then stepped to his feet to survey our work. She gave a slight nod, crossed herself, and turned to leave.

I didn't move.

Honey stopped and turned around, confusion on her face as to why I stood there like a tree.

"I need to see Mama too," I said.

"Oh, yeah. Sorry."

As we walked down the rows, I said, "I don't feel her here. Never did. Just that one time a few weeks ago when I saw her." I chuckled. "Why would they hang out in a cemetery, anyway?"

Honey wasn't ready for humor, and her eyes welled up.

I touched her arm. "I'm sorry. Come on. Let's go."

We wandered along the bayou, throwing out ideas for places that would replace the Talking Tree, but none of them felt right. It really was the perfect spot.

"Maybe it's supposed to be like getting back on a horse," Honey said. "Going to the place where something terrible happened, and over time, it will sting less and less."

The connection Jezebel made between horses and trust bubbled up, but I pushed it down. "I'm not ready for that yet."

"Oh, good." Honey gushed with relief. "I'm so glad. I don't think I could go there either. Not yet. We've got to find somewhere else for now. An escape."

"We could go to Jezebel's," I offered.

Honey stiffened. That would be a no.

We explored most of our side of town, but each candidate for a new meeting place had issues: too busy, nothing to do, not enough shade, no water—or worse, standing water. The list of no's quickly became far longer than even any maybes.

By the end of the day, we found ourselves sitting in the grass in my backyard, close to where Robert used to come and go. It still didn't feel right to be somewhere Robert should be, but it was okay for the rest of our evening, so we sat on the back steps and ate watermelon. Predictable.

That night, as I lay in bed, warmth crept up my leg like from a heating pad, and the bed sank a little near my feet.

Margaret of Thibodaux

Perfume drifted in, and as faint as its fragrance, a lilting, thin soprano sang:

Go to sleepy, little baby.
Go to sleepy, little baby.
When you awake, you'll patty, patty-cake
and ride a shiny little pony.

Chapter 38

Sunday, October 20, 1974

I attended Mass with Honey on a day I needed nothing and I didn't have to go. But Honey needed me, so I did it for her.

It was different, being in the beautiful church without a worry to heave off—sadness still, of course, but that was mine to carry forever. Father Archibald droned on, and my mind wandered to the statues of saints around us. St. Ignatius Loyola. My old friend. Admonishing sinners must be a full-time job, and I realized I was one who needed admonishment too. Well, sometimes.

Honey bumped my arm and angled her head toward Father Archibald.

"Those of you in the congregation who judge others, I advise you to look around at the damage you cause. Gossip is hurtful and unjust. Support of the church does not mean you can make others feel unwanted. The Lamb wants us all."

Father finally stuck up for me, scolding The Fish for their gossip. It would have been nice if he'd done that sooner. It didn't hurt me anymore because I knew for sure it wasn't true. Still, I was grateful for the gesture. Thank you, St. Ignatius.

As usual, I exited the church long before Honey. I still wasn't interested in the ladies' attempts to guilt me into participating in youth group or whatever insufferable activity they came up with. I would sit and listen but I would *not* participate. I would pay more attention to the homily or offer peace to those around me with a firm, kind handshake, but not more than that.

When Honey came out, it struck me that she didn't look the same as she did before Robert died. Maybe she never would. My heart ached thinking of it.

"Let's go to Jezebel's," I said. "She has a swing on her back porch and a big backyard. Sweet tea too." I'd reasoned that if I added benefits and attractions to the offer, Honey might not resist so quickly.

She crossed her arms with a huff. "No."

"Why not?"

"Dunno. Just don't want to. I thought that now that you've seen your mama, you wouldn't need Jezebel anymore."

I turned her comment over in my mind. "I don't *need* her. She's my friend."

"Oh. Never thought of it that way."

We walked in silence. Usually, that provoked Honey to chatter, but not this time. She stayed quiet for longer than I imagined she could. Finally, she said, "Is she kind?"

I skipped a few steps, then turned and skipped backward. "Very."

"What are you doing?"

"Learning to trust."

"Trust? Trust what?"

"Myself. Jezebel says trust is a skill and you have to learn it."

"By skipping?"

"No, silly, by doing something you've never done or doing something you've done that turned out bad. You learn trust. It doesn't just happen."

"I get that we're always learning new things, but—"

"Jezebel says to start with something physical you've never done before. Something simple. Like this." I skipped backward some more. "It's just a stand-in to get my body and brain to act like trust is a thing to be learned. Then, when someone or something needs to be trusted, I know how to go about it."

"Ohhh," Honey said, something clicking in her head. "That's what's really been bothering you. You don't trust Miss Muriel." It wasn't a question.

"I *thought* I didn't trust her. But Jezebel says it's the situation. Mama died, and I felt abandoned. I felt like Robert abandoned me too. I thought everyone would leave me. But I didn't realize it until Mama . . . appeared."

Honey opened her mouth but nothing came out.

"Jezebel's very smart about why people act the way they do."

Honey crossed her arms against anything else Jezebel may have said.

When we arrived at my house, I ran in to change. Five minutes later, I was back.

"Does she make you do voodoo stuff?" Honey asked.

"Annabelle Jane Sinclair. Look at me. Do I look like Jezebel makes me do Vodou things? I'm wearing my same old rolled-up jeans and white shirt. No. The answer is no. Jezebel never even mentioned Vodou after our first meeting. And stop calling it *voodoo*." My voice came out a tiny bit hostile, and I softened my tone at the end.

"I just thought . . ."

"Well, I don't think. I *know*. Jezebel's helped me a lot and I would never talk bad about her. If you don't want to meet her, that's your choice, but you're missing out."

We reached Honey's house before any more questions were tossed my way. While Honey changed, I sniffed the roses on the bushes in the front yard. They were the unscented kind. I'd never noticed that before.

It was still pretty warm out for October, and Honey came bouncing out in a floral dress.

"Now what?" she asked.

The realization hit us both that we didn't know where to go or what to do. All the times before, when we'd done things just the two of us, we'd known Robert was just a call away if we wanted him to join us. Knowing he wasn't anymore was so final.

"Do you want to draw?" I asked.

Honey burst into tears.

"I'm sorry. Don't cry. We don't have to draw."

"It's just—"

"I know," I said needing no explanation. Robert's absence was agonizing, brutal. We both felt it. We didn't have to say it.

We walked around the block as Honey composed herself. "I'm not crying about drawing."

"I know."

"I haven't drawn anything since . . ."

"Nothing?"

"Nothing. I feel like I can't get out of my skin. I want this awful feeling to go away or subside, but it won't. Nothing I do makes it go away. I hate it."

"What if we try something new? Something we've never done before." I looked around us for a clue. "How about . . . knitting?"

Honey pursed her lips and rolled her eyes. "Seriously? Knitting? No."

"Well, at least I'm trying to come up with something. Don't I get points for that?"

"Yes. Two points to Margaret for trying."

It was not like Honey to be sarcastic, and I laughed.

She didn't.

I stopped and took Honey's hand. "I wish I could give you what I know. I wish you could know he's always around."

"It's not good enough. I want him here for real." Honey wiped her face. "I have a cry every morning, but then this dense pressure comes back down on me."

I nodded.

"I wish I'd known this is what it felt like for you all these years. How do you make it better?"

I sighed. "You talk about him. The worst feeling is when folks won't let you talk about him. At first, it's uncomfortable for everyone, but if you always do it, it's like he's just down the street. Not *always*, like it's the only thing you talk about, but always like you talked about him before."

Honey paused for a moment. "I should go talk to his mama. She must want to talk about him too."

We made our way back to my house, where Robert's door was just yards away. I tipped my head toward it. "Go on. She'll be glad you came over."

Honey brightened a bit. "You're the best, Margaret. Thanks."

I watched as she rang the doorbell, then I waved to Mrs. Pennington when she answered the door and invited Honey inside.

Chapter 39

Saturday, March 22, 1975
Five Months Later

I held the nosegay with pink roses and baby's breath at my waist, my Chuck Taylors contrasting the dainty, tea-length tulle and taffeta dress I'd grown to love, and tasted chocolate because of all the pink. As the blue double doors to St. John's Episcopal Church opened wide, I saw Daddy, standing at the altar waiting for Muriel, who was just behind me on the sidewalk. He wasn't used to wearing dress clothes, so although his suit fit perfectly, he kept turning his head and stretching his arms, then fiddling with his navy tie, trying to get it to sit right on his neck. Robert's dad stood next to him. After six years of work by Honey's mother, a pardon from the governor, and a few miracles, he had been released from prison only days ago to be here.

The organist began playing "Jesu, Joy of Man's Desiring."

I turned and smiled at Muriel, ready to accept her and her place in my life, then took a deep breath and headed up the five outside steps that led down the aisle.

The priest had told me last night to walk slowly, to step in time to the music, so I had to concentrate. The Episcopal way of things was more similar to Catholicism than I'd imagined, so I wasn't distracted by an unfamiliar ceremony, but the aisle seemed a thousand yards long.

I stared in awe down the nave, profuse with flowers. The smell was intoxicating, and I breathed it in to savor the fragrance and calm myself. The spare interior of the Episcopal church was such a contrast to the glory and splendor of the Catholic cathedral. It fit Daddy and Muriel, though: small wedding, delightful bride, lucky groom.

The Fish turned in their seats and looked me up and down as they whispered. I enjoyed their stupefied expressions. I especially enjoyed not seeing Mrs. Browner. Daddy's social skewering of inviting all The Fish except her made me grin.

When I finally made it to the front of the church, I took my designated place and surveyed all the faces I recognized. It was the first joyful event since Robert died. But I would not connect death and marriage anymore. Daddy deserved to be happy, and all the attention would now be on Muriel.

Honey sat in the front row next to an empty chair for Robert, adorned with a white ribbon bearing his name, with his mama on the other side. David was behind Honey, along with their folks, and I blushed when I caught him staring at me. On the other side of Honey was Jezebel. I noticed they were holding hands. I didn't have time to think about how or when that connection happened. My part was coming up.

The music changed, and the congregation stood. Muriel appeared in her lovely white dress with a full taffeta skirt, a veil that framed her face, and a bouquet of pink roses, tuberoses, and gardenias. She was not escorted, but no one was missing. She stepped in time to the music, making her linear, forward movement look like a dance. Maybe she *was* an angel, like Mama and Honey said.

Reaching the altar, Muriel stood aligned with Daddy, Mr. Bobby, and me, with the congregation spread before us like a quilt. When the time came for the bride and groom to hold hands, I took the giant bouquet from her, and she winked at me.

The priest's voice was hypnotic and I swayed, steadied only by my fear of dropping the bouquet, not absorbing a word he said. Then, Daddy and Muriel said their vows without mistakes or hesitations, not sounding practiced, though, just sincere. The choir sang, and Daddy hugged Muriel tight and kissed her. The congregation erupted in applause and I joined them as music played the newly married couple back down the aisle.

When my turn came, I linked arms with Mr. Bobby. A comfort, a rightness, crept into my middle and spread like a fever to the rest of me. Robert and Mama were here too.

We all stepped out into the sunshine, giddy with relief and ready to celebrate. "Congratulations!" rang around me and was directed to me. I'd done nothing to warrant congratulations in my understanding of what they were, but the universal response of "Thank you" worked just the same.

When we posed for pictures, I put on my sweetest smile so we didn't have to repeat any. Afterward, I hugged Daddy. "I love you," I said in his ear. "I'm glad you found Muriel."

"I love you, too, Pea. Thanks for being on my side at last."

A group of us moved to the front of the church. As Muriel posed for her solo bridal pictures, Daddy whistled and everyone laughed. When she was finished, Daddy patted my arm and left me to go to his bride.

Honey ambled over with David, Robert's sash draped over her arm, and the edgy nerves returned. "This graveyard is so pretty," she said, referring to the graves behind the church. "There are more trees here, and it's not so crowded."

I ignored David and said to Honey, "Would you like to be here for eternity instead?"

I wasn't sure how the teasing would go over, but she laughed. Then she said, "No, I think that's disallowed, me being Catholic."

I laughed too, grateful for her levity.

"Ride home with us?" she asked. "We'll beat your folks by miles."

Honey called Daddy and Muriel "my folks." It sounded strange, but I guess they were now.

Mr. Sinclair drove us—Mrs. Sinclair, Honey, David, and me—back to our great big house on Legard Street. As we parked in the drive, though, the house suddenly didn't look as big to me as it always had.

The reception was a luncheon, and tables for feasting adorned the living room, parlor, and backyard. A four-seat head table with our ladder-back cane chairs in a neat row held the place of honor in front of our picture window, where I'd been told at the rehearsal to sit beside Muriel. I'd received all the pertinent instructions for today, so I knew where I was supposed to sit, but one cane chair on the far wall drew me to it like I was on the end of a fishing line.

From there, I had a perfect view of the room and everyone in it. I was instantly eight years old again, right after Mama had died. I watched people milling about like I did six years ago. And then I spotted Jezebel. She sat in a cream brocade chair, her bright-flowered dress billowing towards the floor. She raised her teacup in hello.

It was then that it hit me, who the woman in the bright-flowered dress was, the one who had sat in the parlor and later slipped quietly out on the day of Mama's funeral. Tears welled and I pulled a small tissue from my pink glove to dab the corners of my eyes. She'd been there for me all these years without me knowing, letting me come to her when I was ready.

I got up and walked over to her.

"It was you."

"Yes, it's me, baby."

"No. At Mama's funeral. It was you. You sat right there. I always wondered who you were. You were the only one who didn't come talk to me, and I loved you for that."

Jezebel smiled that knowing smile of hers. "Congratulations to you for growing up, Margaret . . . and for gaining a new mama. 'Dat's some'ting to celebrate."

I could not forget Mama, but I would not exclude Muriel.

Jezebel seemed to read my thoughts and patted her lap. I sat down and put my arm around her shoulders.

"You change your mind, no? About Miss Muriel?"

"Yes."

"So?"

"I thought talking to Mama would make a bigger difference than it did. Now I can talk to her, and sometimes, she'll talk back, but she won't interfere unless I ask her."

"'Dat's right."

"No one told me stuff, even important stuff. Not you, not Daddy, not Mama. I had to ask."

Jezebel nodded. "You remember when I said, 'Praying is talking to God and praising Him, while meditation is listening'?" Jezebel smiled as she spoke, and the words came out loving and kind.

"Yes."

"You ever connect 'dose two 'tings? Really 'tink about what I was saying?"

"Obviously not."

"Try it now."

I gathered what I knew, then said out loud, "Praying,

prayer. It's asking. And meditation is listening for an answer. But you never showed me anything about asking. You only said I needed to learn meditation so I could listen."

"Baby, what happens if I tell you to ask but never show you how to get an answer?"

I laughed. "I'd be yelling into the wind. I do that a lot. But I've been learning to listen. I really have."

"I know, and I'm so proud of you. But you had to learn on your own to ask for what your heart desires. Whe'der you're asking God or your Daddy, it's your responsibility to ask . . . not demand, not manipulate, not hope someone will magically understand what you need or want. You have to pray to God, and you have to ask 'de folks in your life." She patted my leg. "So, what you want to ask next?"

I held my breath, afraid to give life to words I might want to kill someday.

"I'm going to ask Muriel if I can call her Mom—when they get back from their honeymoon, of course."

Jezebel pulled back, surprise all over her face. "Is 'dat for you or for her?"

"Both of us, I hope. Start off fresh."

Jezebel put her arms around me and I let her squeeze me tightly.

Honey sidled up to us, grinning like an idiot. "Hold out your hands."

I pulled away from Jezebel and we both did as instructed, my pink gloves perfectly outlining my fingers. Honey dropped sugar cubes into our palms. Jezebel and I both exclaimed

"Ahh" at the same time and popped them into our mouths. Sugar was the best congratulations.

When everyone was seated, before the food was served, it was time for speeches. I'd left my notecards, carefully written out in black ink, on my chair at the head table. I stood from Jezebel's lap and walked gracefully to the table.

I made sure to speak loud enough for everyone to hear me. "Daddy, Miss Muriel. Hi, everyone." I looked around the room and made eye contact with those closest to the head table. "Daddy asked me to give a speech. But what I want to say is more than a speech. It's congratulations, it's an apology, and it's a wish for the future." I turned to Daddy and Muriel. "Congratulations, of course, on your marriage. Also, congratulations on navigating a wedding that involved a teenager—at times, a too-self-involved teenager." Light laughter filled the room. "The apology is for fighting so hard against my world changing. I didn't know it would change for the better with you in it, Muriel. My wish for the future is that our new family has more good times than bad, more love than loss, and more harmony than discord."

I heard guests say "Awww" amongst sniffles, and I waited a few seconds before I continued.

"Daddy, Miss Muriel, I got a lot of things wrong when you told me you were getting married. I couldn't see what was right in front of me, that you loved each other—and me—despite my blowing things up and running away." More laughter. "I've learned a lot in the last few months."

I reached for my champagne glass and noticed yellow

roses on the sideboard, perched in Mama's crystal vase. Muriel caught my eye as she lifted her glass and blew me a kiss.

"To Daddy. To Miss Muriel. To us!" I toasted.

"To us!" Daddy and Muriel repeated.

We feasted on leg of lamb. The Fish had oven-roasted it at the church kitchen and brought it over in three cars—a production in itself. The smell was divine, and I inhaled it into my lungs to affix the memory in my head. It was joined by all the fixins: mashed potatoes swimming in butter, various salads, collard greens. The three-tiered wedding cake with lots of white icing—which was appropriate since white tasted like cake to me—watched over the festivities from the buffet.

After lunch, guests visited with each other, and I walked out to the backyard to sit with Honey and Jezebel. All the planning Muriel had done had paid off. Our yard bloomed with fresh plantings of pink and pale green hothouse hydrangeas, which bowed around a new brick patio Daddy built in February after the last frost. We gathered at one of the tables away from the house, on the grass with a view of the folks talking and laughing. It felt right that laughter came more easily, and I wasn't offended by it anymore.

I looked from Honey to Jezebel and back again. "So, when did this happen?"

"Like I said, what's not to like about Honey?" Jezebel said, patting my hand.

"But you were so dead set against meeting her," I said to Honey.

Honey shrugged with a grin. "I changed my mind. Sometimes that can happen in an instant."

My face lit up in an ear-to-ear smile, elated that two of my favorite people in the world would not require me to pick between them.

David showed up with four plates of cake and set them before Jezebel, Honey, and me. When he set mine down, he brushed against me, and a rush moved up my arm.

"Hope you like cake," he said. "There's gonna be a ton of it left."

I started to take a bite when he added, "Honey, you sure are pretty today . . . and you, Miss Jezebel, striking as always."

A burn of embarrassment flooded my face for being left out. I stared into my lap at my gloves, hoping someone would change the subject. But a moment later, David leaned close to me and said, "I've never seen you so beautiful," and it didn't sound like an afterthought.

I stifled a smile and took a bite of white frosting. I'd thought nothing could be sweeter than plain sugar, but this was. I felt guilty enjoying it in front of Honey, now that she had to moderate her intake, but she seemed unbothered as she took small, ladylike bites.

"They're opening presents!" Mrs. Sinclair called from the back patio door.

We grabbed our cake and David put his free arm around Honey. I'd never seen a brotherly gesture from him in my life, but Honey accepted it as if it were now normal.

Everyone streamed into the parlor, the front living room,

and the foyer to watch as Daddy and Muriel opened their gifts. I'd set mine nearest their chairs, and Muriel reached for it first.

After Muriel had had us over to her house for supper and told me what my name meant, I'd returned the favor and looked up hers. It meant myrrh, the perfume of God, one of the gifts given to Jesus. I hadn't wanted to elevate her with that association before, but it seemed fitting now with all that she was—a gift.

She opened the small blue box and held up the bottle of L'Eau Trois. The name meant "Waters Three," made with myrrh. It had only been released this year and I'd been lucky to find it. Daddy winked at me, and Muriel blew another kiss. I would know Mama and Muriel by their perfumes now. Maybe I already did.

Robert and Mama were present beside me, and Honey moved into the space where I felt Robert. "That was a lovely gift," she said.

"Thanks. I had to think about it a lot. Hope she likes it. Hope Daddy likes it too."

I flashed again to the funeral day and how I prayed for Mama back. Now I had a different mama sitting next to Daddy. It wasn't what I'd meant, but maybe God had answered my prayer in a different way.

By the time the newlyweds set off for Florida, Daddy's Dodge Dart was decorated with tin cans, and the sun sat only inches above the horizon. Folks gathered on the front walk and made a tunnel, throwing handfuls of rice as Daddy and Muriel ran to the car.

We waved as they drove off, and a cool breeze crept into the evening.

We three—Honey on my left, David on my right—each received a kiss on the cheek from Jezebel. "Goodnight," she said, then disappeared down the walk and around the corner.

"Let's go do something," Honey said. "All this sitting has me antsy."

David raised his eyebrows and pointed to himself. "Me too?"

"Why not?" I said, voting that David accompany us.

"All right," David said, rocking on his heels. "Where shall we go this fine evening?"

Honey and I locked eyes and smiled at each other. "Talking Tree," we said in unison.

David cocked his head. "What's that?"

"You'll see," I said as we began to run.

THE END

Acknowledgments

Thank you to Jefferson at First Editing whose insight and skill smoothed the editing path.

Special thanks to my wonderful editor and designer, Stacey Aaronson, who brought this to life in just the way I imagined.

About the Author

Photo credit: Linda Blue Photography

JO TAYLOR is an obstreperous, retired ER Nurse who is likely an obstreperous writer too. She grew up with three stepmothers (not at the same time), and is a pragmatic psychic/medium, fascinated by everything woo. She's lived on a boat and traced her genealogy back to the year 310 (maybe, probably, you know how genealogy is). She's been married for thirty-three years, and all her hero characters are based on her husband, a hero in real life. Her first book, *Postcards: Collected Poems and Short Stories* came out in July 2024. *Margaret of Thibodaux* is her first novel.

Follow Jo online at:

jotaylorauthor.substack.com

jotaylorauthor.com • x.com/jotaylorauthor

Made in the USA
Middletown, DE
05 May 2025

75178960R00181